THE CON MAN

Elmer Myers has nursed Mammoth Pictures into becoming the second-largest picture-making corporation in Hollywood. But for the last three years, mysterious accidents have held up the completion of his films, until all the profits have been eaten up in overheads. Now Myers has borrowed heavily, staking everything on the making of an expensive super-epic to restore his fortunes. But when his film editor is murdered and the only negative of the completed film stolen, Myers realises he has a deadly enemy intent on his ruination . . .

GERALD VERNER

THE CON MAN

Complete and Unabridged

LINFORD
Leicester

First published in Great Britain

First Linford Edition
published 2015

A catalogue record for this book is available
from the British Library.

ISBN 978–1–4448–2449–0

Published by
F. A. Thorpe (Publishing)
Anstey, Leicestershire

Set by Words & Graphics Ltd.
Anstey, Leicestershire
Printed and bound in Great Britain by
T. J. International Ltd., Padstow, Cornwall

This book is printed on acid-free paper

1

Mr. Myers is Confidential

Mr. Elmer Myers rolled a long black cigar from one corner of his thin-lipped mouth to the other and looked across the table at his companion.

'I am banking everything on this picture,' he said in his pleasant husky voice, 'everything, Frank. You understand? It's just got to be the biggest thing ever presented to the public.'

Frank Leyland crushed out the stub of his cigarette in his plate and nodded. He was tall and slim, in direct contrast to the short fatness of the man seated opposite him. The black hair, grey at the temples, framed an eager face that was lean without being thin, and gave the impression of enormous vitality. Everything about Frank Leyland radiated life. His hands were never still for long, and his eyes, when they spoke of even the most trivial detail, were alive with enthusiasm. It was many years since he had left England to make good in Hollywood. His reputation as one of the most imaginative of the younger directors was due in a great measure to his enormous capacity for being interested in everything.

'The picture should be a winner,' he declared. 'So far as I can see, it ought to make film history. Floyd Elliott's script is the best I've read in years — and that's saying something. He's put everything he ever knew — and a lot I didn't think he knew — in that story, and it's some story.'

Mr. Myers thoughtfully picked his teeth with a gold toothpick.

'When'll you start shootin'?' he asked.

'Next Wednesday,' answered Leyland. 'The interior sets are all completed and the models for the others are almost finished. In fact we could take the stage tomorrow if Rita Harlow were free.'

Mr. Myers grunted.

'She'll finish the picture she's making for R.I.A. on Tuesday,' he said. 'See here, Frank, you'll have to watch her, she's temperamental. She's got a habit of going all 'arty' in the middle of a picture and holding up the works.'

The eagle-faced director smiled.

'You can't tell me anything about Rita Harlow I don't know,' he replied. 'This film she's doing now is the only one in which I haven't directed her personally.'

'I know that,' said Elmer Myers. 'That's why I engaged you to make this 'super' of ours. I'm only warning you, Frank, and I'm naturally a bit anxious. I've sunk every penny we've got, and borrowed a lot more from the bank for this picture and it's got to be finished according to schedule. It's the last shot in the locker. It's either going to make or break us. We've had a hell of a lot of bad luck lately, and if this picture does not get over, Mammoth Picture Corporation Inc. will go bust, and it'll be some bust.'

Leyland raised his rather thick eyebrows. 'Bad as that?' he said.

'Yes, sir, as bad as that and worse,' declared Myers, nodding his large head. 'But I think this film will put us on our feet again. It's costin' a lot of money — over a million dollars — to make, but it's got the finest story and the finest cast that ever came out of Hollywood, and I'm going to put it over with the biggest boom of publicity that the world's ever heard of. It's going to make the whole country sit up and goggle! But — ' He leaned forward, took his cigar from between his lips, and wagged it impressively at the man opposite him. ' — we can't afford any hitches or accidents, or anything like that. There ain't a penny margin to play with.'

Leyland frowned.

'So far as I'm concerned,' he replied, 'everything will be OK, but you're taking a big risk, Elmer.'

'I know I am,' answered his companion, 'and I'm playing for a big stake. I've kinda got a soft spot in my heart for Mammoth Pictures. You see, I was in on the ground floor and founded the company before the boom, when motion pictures were more of a novelty than an entertainment. The studio then was a barn, and the offices and developing room a miner's hut. There were no stars then, no publicity men, no nothing. And I've nursed it and watched it grow, Frank, from what it was then to what it is now. The second largest picture-making corporation in Hollywood. I've watched Los Angeles, Beverley Hills and Culver City, and all the rest of the colony grow up round it, and I've watched it grow up with 'em. A few years ago, before the talkies came in, and blew the old industry to bits, Mammoth Pictures were making a profit of over fifteen million dollars a year, now they're not making fifteen million cents.' He stopped and took a gulp of the large glass of orange juice in front of him. 'For the last three years everything I've touched has gone wrong,' he went on. 'Pictures have been started and accident upon accident has held up their completion, until all the profits there might have been have got eaten up in overheads. That's why I'm telling you, this picture's got to be finished within its schedule.'

'You can bank on me to do my part,' said Leyland. 'You've certainly had a run of bad luck.'

Elmer Myers looked at him and his

eyes narrowed to slits. He opened his mouth to speak, said nothing, glanced quickly round the crowded restaurant, and then apparently making up his mind, hitched his chair closer to the table and leaned across until his large head was almost touching his companion's.

'I'm not so sure that it was all bad luck,' he said in a low hoarse whisper. 'I guess a lot of it was a deliberate attempt on somebody's part to break me.'

Frank Leyland's face changed to an expression of amazement.

'Are you serious — ' he began incredulously.

'I'll say I am,' interrupted Myers. 'Don't talk so loud.' The film director dropped his voice to the level of the others.

'But,' he said, 'who would attempt to do such a thing, Elmer? Everybody likes you — '

'Oh, it's not a personal matter,' said the other quickly. 'If I'm right, it's just a matter of business — dirty business if you like — but, well, with some people the word 'business' covers a multitude of sins.' He shrugged his broad shoulders.

The astonishment on Frank's face remained.

'Do you mean somebody's trying to force you to shut up shop?' he asked a little sceptically.

Myers nodded slowly several times, and his big face was grave.

'Four times during the past three years,' he said, 'Oscar Levenstein has made me an offer for the whole concern, lock, stock and barrel.'

Frank Leyland uttered a low prolonged whistle.

'I see,' he murmured, and he did.

Oscar Levenstein was the managing director of the largest picture-making unit in Hollywood. World Wide Films turned out fifty per cent more pictures than any other studio in the colony. They turned them out on the mass-production principle, substituting quantity for quality, and flooding the market. The capital behind the concern was colossal and the profits huge. They had a monopoly of the most popular stars and kept a contingent of writers permanently under contract. It was Levenstein who during the silent days introduced the iniquitous block booking system, working through Consolidated Renters, a firm of film distributors that was an offshoot of the parent company and controlled by Levenstein himself. It was an open secret that World Wide Films wanted to enlarge their studios and plant. Everybody knew it from Los Angeles to Culver City. The big straggling block of buildings that housed the company lay at the foot of Beverley Hills, cheek by jowl with Elmer Myers's smaller and more compact unit. Any contemplated extension would necessarily embrace the latter's property.

'So you think that it's Levenstein who's trying to freeze you out?' muttered Leyland after a pause.

'I do,' answered Myers. 'Over and over again his solicitors have approached me with tempting offers. Six months ago Levenstein himself asked me to lunch and suggested as things were so bad I should sell out. I politely told him to go to the devil, and he said, with that slow one-sided smile of his, that before I was very much older I should have to sell to him, and would be only too glad to accept any offer he might like to make.'

He took another cigar from his pocket and bit off the end viciously.

Leyland pursed his lips.

'I can hardly believe Levenstein would go to the lengths you suggest,' he said, shaking his head. 'I don't like the man — nobody does — but it's difficult to believe that he's such a scoundrel as you imply.'

Myers lit his cigar, flicked the match into an ashtray, and blew out a cloud of smoke.

'I've not an atom of proof myself,' he said. 'For that reason I've never mentioned my suspicions to anyone else. But the series of accidents didn't start until I turned down Levenstein's second offer.' He contemplated the end of his cigar to see that it was burning evenly. 'I don't know why I've mentioned this to you at all,' he went on. 'I reckon possibly because this picture we're makin' means so much, and I want to put you on your guard. Anyway, I hope you'll keep what I said to yourself.'

'I'm not likely to spread it around,' said Frank Leyland, 'and I'm glad you've told me. It's good to get a thing like that off your chest.'

He beckoned one of the numerous beautiful girls who, coming to Hollywood with visions of stardom and fame, had been forced to seek work as waitresses in order to live in that city of beauty and heartbreak.

'We may as well get along and inspect the model of the street set,' he said as he paid the bill. 'Blane said it would be finished this morning.'

Myers agreed, and the two men left the Brown Derby where they had been lunching, that quaintly-named and famous restaurant on the Wilshire Boulevard, which is built in the shape of a bowler hat, and getting into Myers's car, were driven towards the offices of the Mammoth Picture Corporation Inc.

They continued to talk over the coming film as the car sped over the well-kept boulevards in the direction of Culver City. The studios of the Mammoth Picture Corporation lay back from the road and were

10

approached by a wide highway lined on either side with palm trees. As the driver of the car turned into this he increased his speed, for there was very little traffic.

'I'm getting out a publicity scheme for this picture that'll knock the world,' said Mr. Myers. 'I tell you, Frank, that we're going to clean up a packet, unless — '

He broke off as with a screaming of brakes the car came to a sudden standstill and almost jerked him through the glass of the window which divided the interior from the driver.

'What the heck!' he exclaimed angrily as he recovered his balance. 'Why did Wilson pull up like that for? The man must have gone clean crazy!'

'I think there's something the matter,' said Frank Leyland quickly.

He had caught sight of the chauffeur's white face as that agitated man got down from the driving seat and came round to the door.

'I should think there was something,' grunted Mr. Myers wrathfully, 'and there might have been something far worse the matter — '

He was interrupted by the hurried opening of the door and the appearance of the chauffeur's head.

'Do you mind getting out, sir?' said the man in a voice that trembled slightly. 'I think there's been an accident.'

'Accident? What do you mean?' said Mr. Myers, hoisting his fat body with difficulty from the cushions of the seat and stepping down into the roadway.

'That's what I mean, sir,' said the chauffeur and pointed. 'Look!'

Elmer Myers followed the direction of his finger and saw the crumpled-up body of a man lying by the sidewalk.

'Good heavens!' he exclaimed, his voice full of concern. 'The poor guy looks as though he's been run over. Come on, Frank, he may not be dead. We'd better see if we can do anything.'

He trotted over to the motionless figure, followed by Frank Leyland and the chauffeur. Bending down, he peered into the upturned face, and the next second he had started back with a strangled cry.

'Good God!' he muttered in a husky whisper. 'It's Lee Collins!'

'What?' Frank Leyland was at his side in a moment. 'Great Scott, so it is!' he exclaimed breathlessly.

Mr. Myers, his face white and haggard, strove to speak calmly.

'Is he — dead?' he whispered.

Leyland stooped over the man in the roadway.

'I'm afraid he is,' he said in a hushed whisper. 'It looks as if a car or something has knocked him down.'

He indicated the torn clothing and the ugly gash that ran from temple to chin, and from which the blood had oozed sluggishly, forming a little pool in the dusty roadway around the head. Elmer Myers frowned and his fingers tightened on the remains of his cigar.

'We'd better go on to the studios,' he said, 'and phone for a doctor. You stay here, Wilson.'

The chauffeur nodded, and without another word Mr. Myers turned and began to walk swiftly towards the big gate leading to the Mammoth Pictures studios, which was barely two hundred yards along on the right-hand side. He spoke

13

only once, and then it was more to himself than to Frank Leyland.

'Poor Collins,' he said below his breath, and again, 'poor Collins.'

They passed in through a side gate, and along a semicircular strip of gravel drive to the entrance. As they ascended the steps the timekeeper came out of a glass-sided office just inside the vestibule.

'Glad you're back, Mr. Myers,' he said. 'Mr. Phillips has been looking for you . . .'

'I can't see him — I can't see anybody!' broke in Elmer Myers shortly. 'Get on the 'phone to Dr. Paterson, and tell him to rush round here as soon as you can. There's been an accident.'

'An accident?' the timekeeper looked at him curiously,

'Yes, Mr. Collins has been killed.' And then as the man's mouth gaped open: 'Don't stand there staring, man, get on the phone!'

The timekeeper hurried to obey and they heard his voice calling a number. The film magnate waited impatiently until he returned.

'Dr. Paterson's coming round at once, sir,' he said.

Mr. Myers nodded.

'Good!' he said briefly; 'has Mr. Stanwyck come back from lunch?'

The timekeeper shook his head.

'Not yet, sir,' he answered.

'Ask him to wait for me in my office; I want to see him,' ordered his employer. 'Come along, Frank; we'll go back to Wilson and wait to hear what the doctor has to say.'

His face was stern and set as he walked back down the gravel drive towards the gates.

'Lee Collins,' he said slowly and distinctly. 'The best cameraman for process shots in the whole of America — dead! The accidents have started again, Frank.'

There was a peculiar expression in Frank Leyland's eyes as he met the steady brown ones of the other.

'You — you don't think it was an accident?' he said.

Elmer Myers stopped dead and faced him.

'No, sir, I don't!' he cried. 'Somebody

15

wanted to make sure that Collins wouldn't turn for us; somebody thought it would delay the picture being taken, knowing that we can't afford delay, so they ran him down. Well, they're going to be disappointed. We're going to make that picture, Frank, in spite of everything they can do, and, by heck, we're going to make it on time!'

2

The Stranger

The shooting of Mammoth Pictures' super-film began to time and continued to grow day by day without further accident. The strained look on the fat face of Mr. Elmer Myers gradually faded, and was replaced by one of complacent satisfaction. For the rushes, which he viewed daily in the small private projecting theatre attached to the studio, exceeded even his expectations. The place of Collins, the cameraman, had been taken by a German expert, especially rushed over by air from Germany, who, according to the verdict of Frank Leyland, was 'the goods'. Even Rita Harlow had shown no sign of giving way to an outburst of temperament, and everything was proceeding smoothly, with the result that Mr. Myers's face became wreathed in smiles.

At a time when the film was nearing completion there came to Los Angeles a stranger. He came on the Chief, the wonder train that covers the thousands of miles separating Los Angeles from Chicago in just under five days.

He came unheralded and unmet, for he was neither a famous personage nor known to anyone in the film city. Tall, slim and good-looking, he was a man who at first glance looked youthful, but who on closer inspection proved older than he seemed. There was a touch of silver behind his ears, and the hard expression in the dark eyes, and the tiny lines about the thin mouth contradicted that first impression of boyishness.

At a rough estimate his age might have been anything between thirty-five and fifty — as a matter of fact it was midway — but he walked with the swing of youth. He was not an American; his drawling, well-bred voice had the stamp of Oxford, and his clothes had obviously been built by a Savile Row expert.

Together with his considerable and label-covered luggage he was driven through the straggling streets and boulevards of Los Angeles to the Beverley Wilshire, that extremely select hotel that almost faces the Brown Derby and caters for the discriminating visitors to the world film centre.

A suite had evidently been reserved for him, for the reception clerk greeted him with a smiling welcome when he mentioned his name and rang for a page while he signed the register. His signature was in keeping with his appearance: boldly black in thick heavy up-and-down strokes, it stood out from the page for all the world to see. 'Captain Garvin Chase, London, England.'

And yet this pleasant and distinguished-looking man who presently followed the obsequious page to the waiting lift had once stood in the dock at the Old Bailey and listened to the scathing remarks of the judge who had sent him down for seven years for fraud.

Had Detective Inspector Shadgold of Scotland Yard been there he would have given quite another name to the man who had signed himself Captain Garvin Chase with such a flourish. A name that was a little less high-sounding and more plebeian. The quiet Inspector Leekin, who had charge of the record office, and who methodically spent his life filing the history of known criminals, could have added several more names. For the card bearing details of Captain Garvin Chase's career also bore a string of aliases heading the neatly typed dossier: Thomas Spearman, a Tommy the Black, a Gentleman Tom, etc., etc. There was, however, no mention of Captain Garvin Chase, and this was not surprising, for the gentleman who called himself by that grandiloquent name had only acquired it in a moment of inspiration during the last three weeks.

He expressed complete approval with the luxuriant suite that had been placed at his disposal and ordered a syphon of soda. When this had been brought and the waiter had gone he unpacked a flask of brandy from his suitcase and poured himself out a drink.

With the glass in his hand he strolled over to the window and looked thoughtfully out at the view that lay before him.

The view was worth looking at. Three miles away, beyond the foreground of shops and drug stores, filling stations and agents' offices that line the Wilshire Boulevard, rose the slope of the Beverley Hills, bathed in the golden sunlight which is California's greatest asset, and dotted with the picturesque white houses in which the stars of filmdom live and have their being.

The air was marvellously clear, and tasted to the man who stood breathing it by the open window like a draught of vintage champagne. And yet it is doubtful if he saw very much of the beautiful view that stretched before him and the opulent cars that passed back and forth in the street beneath. For Thomas Spearman was a materialist, and the evidence of the golden material his soul craved surrounded him on every side.

He had come to Hollywood with no settled plan, but he was an opportunist and a great believer in luck. Here he was in the middle of wealth, and if his quick brain could not find some way of transferring a large portion of it to his own pocket, then the fault was his.

He pulled out a roll of bills and flipped them over with his long fingers. Fifteen hundred dollars — his entire fortune. The total was disconcerting, and he frowned and pursed his lips. This would not last him very long; some scheme for replenishing the exchequer would have to be put into action at the soonest possible moment. He turned from the window as the hotel valet came softly into the room to unpack his things and poured himself out another drink.

'Leave out the grey flannels and turn me on a hot bath,' he ordered as the man carried his suitcase into the bedroom.

'Certainly, sir.' The valet bowed and retired into the inner room, and Mr. Spearman, alias Captain Garvin Chase, lit a cigarette and smoked thoughtfully until the servant returned to announce that the bath was ready.

Dismissing the man, he went into the bedroom and began leisurely to undress. Two minutes later he was lying up to his neck in hot water, gazing through the steam with half-closed eyes at the ceiling.

But his lazy expression was not in keeping with his thoughts, for his alert brain was toying with future plans for his financial benefit. At the end of five minutes he took a cold shower, and as the water beat an icy tattoo on his body his thin lips curled into a smile, for he had evolved three possible schemes for his attack on Hollywood's wealth. They were only in the embryo stage, but from past experience Mr. Spearman knew the details would be developed almost subconsciously.

He began humming a little tune as he dried himself, and he was still humming it when he passed into his bedroom and began to dress. At a quarter to one he descended the stairs to the lounge, a cool, well-groomed figure in silver-grey.

A waiter brought him a glass of orange juice, and as he sipped it rather unappreciatively — his natural inclination was for something stronger — he glanced languidly about him.

The lounge only held a smattering of people, for there were not many visitors at the Beverley Wilshire at that time of year.

Mr. Spearman, however, allowed his eyes to rest for a fraction of a second on two fat and expensively dressed American gentlemen, and he mentally noted them as the type who might probably be useful.

He lunched carefully but sparingly, and in the afternoon went for a walk to survey the ground. In the evening, immaculately attired in a beautifully cut dinner suit, he sauntered across to the Brown Derby at which he had previously booked a table for dinner.

The place was crowded, as it usually is. Faces which had become common in the newspapers of the world were to be seen on every side, and after he had selected his dinner with great care and given his order, Mr. Spearman leaned back in his chair and surveyed the scene about him with the eye of a connoisseur.

Here were people whose weekly earnings would, to use Mr. Spearman's mental expression, put him 'on velvet' for many months. Here were riches which, by the exercise of a little ingenuity, might be side-tracked into his own pocket.

As he slowly ate the beautifully cooked

food that was presently brought to him a feeling of pleasurable contentment stole over him. The world, or rather this part of it in which he found himself, was his oyster. An oyster which, to judge from his surroundings, held a considerable number of pearls.

Nobody knew better than Mr. Spearman that the oyster is a notoriously difficult thing to open except by an expert. But then he had spent the greater part of his life in opening oysters with varying degrees of success, and Mr. Spearman watched. And then one man suddenly glanced at his watch and rose to his feet.

He called the waitress, hurriedly paid his bill, and with a little man following at his heels, went swiftly out of the restaurant. Mr. Spearman also rose, and skinning a bill from the roll in his pocket laid it on the table. As he made his way towards the exit he passed the girl who had served him, and murmuring that she could keep the change, went out quickly in the wake of the others.

He saw them walking along the Wilshire Boulevard in the direction of

Culver City. For a moment he hesitated, and then with an imperceptible shrug of his shoulders he started to follow. Apparently they had no suspicion that they were being shadowed, for they never once looked round, but continued on their way until they reached North Maple Drive.

They turned into this wide and pleasant residential thoroughfare, which is lined on either side by the picturesque villas of the more wealthy of Hollywood's residents, and went on until they came to the drive gates of a big house three-quarters of the way up on the right-hand side.

Here the taller man paused, said something to his companion, and they passed through the entrance.

Mr. Spearman had had to walk quickly to keep them in sight, but now he slowed and his brows drew together in a frown. Should he follow them and try to learn what had brought them to this big and pretentious-looking house, or should he go back to his hotel? He decided to try and learn a little more than he knew already.

It has been stated that Mr. Spearman

was an opportunist and a great believer in luck. He believed that here fate had thrown in his way an opportunity which if he followed it up would prove advantageous. Discretion whispered to him to be careful, but he turned a deaf ear to the whisper, and, turning in through the wide gates, began to make his way cautiously up the well-kept drive.

Two hours later he came back, and as he walked swiftly down the Wilshire Boulevard in the direction of his hotel there was a smile on his face.

For quite by accident that night Mr. Spearman had stumbled on a piece of information that, handled properly, he considered would put a fortune in his pocket and make him independent for the rest of his life.

3

The Scheme

Mr. Oscar Levenstein was a man who liked the good things of life. From the time when forty years previously he had worked outward from the small and dirty top-floor garret in a mean street in the Bowery his mind had held only one objective, and that was to acquire as easily and with as little effort as possible the money that would supply him with the luxuries his microscopic soul craved.

And at the age of fifty-two he had achieved his mission. Given a certain ruthlessness and an entire disregard for the feelings of others, no conscience and a willingness to use every means, legal and otherwise, it is not difficult to amass a considerable fortune. And Mr. Levenstein possessed all these attributes. He had risen to his present position as managing director and virtual owner of the biggest picture-making corporation in Hollywood by trampling underfoot every decent instinet.

The trail of his success was marked by ruined homes and broken hearts; the deaths of at least three men could be indirectly traced to the result of Mr. Levenstein's business acumen. But this disturbed his peace of mind not at all. He was a man who seldom looked back. All his attention was concentrated on the forward march. The dazzling golden beacon that glittered in the darkness of his soul was the only thing that mattered.

He was a rich man — even in that city of wealth this was openly acknowledged — but he was the type that could never be rich enough. In the old days he had craved dollars; when dollars came to him he wanted hundreds; when he got hundreds he set his mind on thousands. So the vicious circle went on.

Sitting at the great desk in the luxuriously furnished study of his house on North Maple Drive, he was an unprepossessing figure. Considerably below medium height, his fat little legs barely touched the carpet. His bloated body, flabby and unhealthy from overindulgence, filled and overflowed the padded chair. His enormous head, bald save for a fringe of grey-black hair, seemed to grow out of his chest, for his neck was so short and fat that it was scarcely discernible. He was a man of many chins, and an unhealthy skin that was leaden-hued and repellent, His mouth, small and over-red, was almost obscured in the folds of his puffy cheeks, and his eyes, deep-sunk beneath hairless brows, had the hard glitter which can be seen in the eyes of a snake.

Yet in spite of his physical drawbacks he radiated a certain power. He was smoking a cigar and frowning thought-fully at the blotting pad in front of him, when there came a tap on the door and a footman entered. He advanced noiselessly over the thick pink carpet and presented the contents of a salver for his master's inspection. Mr. Levenstein glanced at the card, grunted and removed the cigar from his lips.

'Show Mr. Guinan in,' he said, and his voice was a surprise and a revelation, for it was deep-toned and melodious, with a rich timbre which would have done credit to a leading actor.

Mr. Levenstein was very proud of his voice. He had, in fact, carefully cultivated it. On more than one occasion it had succeeded in charming several thousands of dollars out of the pockets of his victims to his own.

The footman withdrew, and presently came back ushering in two visitors.

'Good evening, Mr. Guinan,' said Mr. Levenstein, addressing the taller of the two men, but making no effort to rise. 'Sit down, will you?'

He nodded casually towards two easy chairs drawn up in front of the huge flat-topped desk. Lefty Guinan gave a quick glance round, mentally appraising the richness and quality of the room, and lounged over to the chair which his host had indicated. He waited until the footman had gone out and closed the door, and then he introduced his companion.

'This is Spike Munro,' he said with a jerk of his head towards the man who had come in with him. 'I've brought him along because maybe he'll be useful. He's worked with me before.'

'You know your own business best,' said Mr. Levenstein noncommittally. 'Have you told him anything about the scheme?'

'I've told him as much as I know myself,' answered Guinan, 'which isn't very much. He knows that we're here to crab the making of this new picture you told me about.'

'Then he knows more than I do,' interrupted Mr. Levenstein. 'Because you're not here for that purpose at all!'

Lefty Guinan looked at him in astonishment.

'But say,' he protested, 'what's the big idea? That's what you told me when we talked in Chicago. You had some scheme of starting a fire — '

'Whatever ideas I may have had then,' said Mr. Levenstein, before he could complete the sentence, 'you can forget. I've struck a much better plan.'

'Oh, I see.' There was a note of relief in Guinan's voice. 'I thought for the moment that the whole thing was off, and we'd come all the way from Chicago for nothin'. What's the new scheme?'

Mr. Levenstein dropped the butt of his cigar into a large ashtray, pulled a silver box towards him and carefully selected another. It was characteristic of him that he made no attempt to offer the box to his two guests.

'The new scheme,' he said slowly, when the cigar was alight and burning evenly, 'is much simpler and more effective than a fire or anything else I can think of. The fire, I think, would be rather clumsy and would inevitably destroy the property. A thing which I don't want to do if it can be avoided.' He glanced quickly round the room as though to assure himself there were no eavesdroppers. 'My object, as you know, is to smash Mammoth Pictures so that I can acquire the property for a song. I wouldn't even mind paying its market value if Myers would sell, but he won't. The only way I can get it is to break him.' His voice was even and without emotion. He might have been discussing any ordinary business proposition, which, according to his own peculiar code, he was. 'He's spent every penny he can lay his hands on for this picture,' he went on, 'and is deeply in debt with the banks as well. The trade show has been fixed and duly advertised. If that picture is not forthcoming — ' He shrugged his shoulders. ' — well, that's the end of Myers and Mammoth Pictures.'

Lefty Guinan moved impatiently in his chair.

'You're thinking ahead of me, boss,' he said, shaking his head. 'I know all this you're tellin' me. You said the same thing in Chicago. The question is: What do you want us to do?'

Mr. Levenstein's hard eyes regarded him coldly,

'I'm coming to that, if you'll kindly refrain from interrupting me,' he said.

Lefty Guinan muttered an apology.

'When a picture is completed,' said the man behind the big desk after a pause, 'it's in the form of a negative, like an ordinary still photograph. From this negative a print is made to be sent to the cutting room to be cut and edited. That is to say, the scenes, which are all numbered, are put in their right order or altered at the discretion of the editor and the director. At this stage of the proceedings there is — with the exception of the daily rushes, which are short lengths of film printed daily from the negative for the convenience of the director so that he can see how his work is progressing — only one print of the film in existence. The one on which the cutter is working.' He leaned slightly forward. 'If this and the negative were stolen there would be nothing left but to take the picture all over again.'

Guinan drew in his breath with a long soft hiss.

'I get you,' he breathed. He shot a quick glance at the silent man by his side. 'You want us to steal the film?'

Mr. Levenstein nodded.

'Exactly,' he said gently. 'Simple, isn't it? But I assure you very effective. If that negative and the print which the cutters are working on, together with the rushes should be stolen and — destroyed, Mammoth Pictures would be finished. They haven't got sufficient capital to make the film over again.'

'I'll say it's a stroke of genius,' said Lefty Guinan admiringly.

'It's a good stroke of business,' grunted Mr. Levenstein. 'Now, then, here's my proposition. Deliver that negative and print into my hands and I'll give you fifty thousand dollars.'

Guinan's faded blue eyes brightened greedily.

'Fifty per cent, on account,' he said, 'and it's OK with me.'

Mr. Levenstein blew out a cloud of smoke.

'You shall have twenty-five thousand dollars in cash tomorrow morning,' he agreed.

'Why not a cheque now?' suggested Mr. Spike Munro, speaking for the first time.

'Don't be a fool,' said Levenstein without heat. 'Do you think I'm going to give you anything which could be traced back to me? If you do, think again! I've got nothing to do with this business, you understand — nothing whatever.'

'That's OK with me,' said Lefty

Guinan, and Mr. Spike Munro grunted an assent. 'The job shouldn't be so very difficult, but I shall want some information. How do I know I've got hold of the right film?'

'You can tell by the title,' replied Mr. Levenstein. 'It's called *The Man-God*. Do you understand anything about photography?'

Guinan nodded.

'Well, then, you'll be able to distinguish which is the negative.'

'Where do they keep the thing?' asked Lefty Guinan.

'In a safe in the laboratory,' said the man behind the desk. 'Come here.'

He pulled open a drawer and brought out a sheet of paper. Spreading this out on the blotting-pad in front of him, he picked up a gold pencil, and as Lefty Guinan got up and went round the desk to his side he began with quick light strokes to sketch a plan of the Mammoth Studios. 'Here are the general offices,' he said, as his hand moved swiftly over the blank paper. 'Here's the projecting theatre, to the left here is a corridor ending in an iron door. You'll have difficulty with that — it's always kept locked and it's pretty strong.'

'I think I shall be able to manage it all right,' said Guinan with a confident smile.

'Well, that's your business.' Mr. Levenstein went on sketching his plan. 'Beyond the door is the laboratory and printing room. The safe is here.' He marked the position with a rough square. 'This door leads from the laboratory to the stock-room, and this other one to the cutting room. The fire escape runs up the back of the building here to a door which opens into the laboratory secured by a panic bolt. Is that clear?'

'Clear as daylight,' said Lefty Guinan. 'There's a night watchman, of course?'

'There are two,' said Mr. Levenstein. 'You'll have to deal with them, but don't go too far if you can avoid it.'

'Trust me.' Guinan winked. 'I cut my eye-teeth in this game, mister.'

He picked up the rough plan that Mr. Levenstein had drawn, folded it and put it in his pocket.

'One last question,' he said. 'When do

you want us to go after this film?'

'I'll let you know that,' answered Mr. Levenstein. 'At the present moment they're shooting the final scene. Where are you staying?'

'We haven't fixed anywhere yet,' said Lefty Guinan. 'I don't know this burg at all. I thought perhaps you'd be able to recommend somewhere.'

Mr. Levenstein thought for a moment.

'You'd better stay at Mack's,' he said. 'It's a little hotel-restaurant just outside Los Angeles. Not a pretentious place, but quite comfortable.'

'Then I think we'll get along there now,' said Lefty Guinan, glancing at his watch. 'I'll call you up in the morning and let you know if we're fixed there, and you can send the cash along.'

'You'll get it before the evening,' said Mr. Levenstein, and his tone suggested that the interview was over.

Lefty Guinan and the silent Spike Munro took their leave, and for a long time after they had gone Mr. Levenstein sat on, his flabby, unpleasant-looking face wearing a complacent smile.

* ★ *

The smile would not have been so complacent if he could have heard the conversation between the two men who had just left him. Until halfway along the Wilshire Boulevard neither of them had spoken, then it was Lefty Guinan who broke the silence.

'I see stacks of bucks ahead,' he said softly.

Mr. Munro grunted.

'Fifty thousand dollars is a lot, but I wouldn't call it stacks,' he growled.

'I wasn't thinking of fifty thousand dollars,' replied Lefty Guinan. 'Handled properly, there's more in it for us than that, Spike.' Spike looked up at his companion.

'Spill it,' he said briefly.

'If this fellow Levenstein is willing to pay fifty thousand dollars to us to pinch him that film,' said Mr. Guinan slowly, 'how much do you suppose the Mammoth Picture Corporation Inc. would pay us to get it back again?'

Mr. Munro stopped dead.

'Lefty,' he said, and there was admiration in his hoarse voice, 'you've got a brain!'

'Brains are my speciality,' retorted the gratified Mr. Guinan. 'We're goin' to clear up a lot of money, Spike, on this deal — a lot of money.'

Curiously enough, at that moment Mr. Thomas Spearman, lying at ease between the soft sheets in his comfortable bed at the Beverley Wilshire, was thinking exactly the same thing.

4

The Quarrel

In any other city than Hollywood Mary Henley would have attracted a second glance. In that centre of feminine loveliness, however, she was just a beautiful girl among many others. She was slim and fair with the creamy-rose complexion that goes with natural fairness, for neither Mary's complexion nor her hair owed anything to artifice. As she sat at a small table in one of the cheaper restaurants she offered a striking contrast to her companion. Irene Claremont was beautiful, too, but it was a dark beauty, and the redness of her lips came from a small tube that she carried in her handbag, and her dead white skin could be purchased at two and sixpence a bottle.

'I heard they wanted somebody my type,' said Mary, dropping the match with which she had just lit her cigarette into her saucer, and addressing the man who sat opposite to her. 'I was at the studio directly it opened in the morning, but do you know there were already crowds of girls waiting and the man at the door told me they had fixed.'

Dick Rennit nodded sympathetically.

'I know,' he said. 'The first breath of a job and there's always thousands buzzing round, like flies round a jam pot.'

'The unemployment's terrible,' murmured Irene. 'Simply terrible. Thousands of extras are literally starving.'

'We're not far off it, my dear,' said Mary with a grimace. 'I must get a job somewhere; I've only got two dollars in the world.'

On the strength of winning a beauty competition arranged by a London daily she had come to Hollywood eighteen months previously, full of hope and ambition — and seventy-five pounds. The hope and ambition still remained.

'The place is overcrowded, that's the trouble,' said Dick Rennit, who gained a precarious livelihood by doing any and every job that happened to be going. 'People flock to Hollywood full of the glamour and fame, and an easy living. More illusions must have been killed here than in any other place on the earth.'

'Well, I'm going after a job as a waitress this afternoon,' declared Mary Henley. 'One of the girls at the Brown Derby was telling me that there was a vacancy.'

'You'd better keep it to yourself,' warned Irene. 'If it leaks out the place will be besieged before you can get there.'

There was a little silence, and then Dick said suddenly:

'How was it you didn't get into Mammoth Pictures' latest? I thought Lamont was going to fix it?'

Mary reddened, and Irene noticing the flush looked at her sharply.

'He was,' she said hesitantly, 'but, well, the conditions made it impossible for me to accept.'

'Oh, I see.' Dick nodded understandingly. 'Like that was it? Lamont's got a reputation for that sort of thing.'

'He — he — was beastly,' said Mary angrily.

'Try to pull over the love stuff, did he?' said Irene. 'He's like that, tried it with me once.'

'And you fell,' said Dick with a chuckle. 'Six months ago you were crackers about him.'

Irene frowned.

'I was nothing of the sort,' she declared. 'I strung him along because I thought he might be useful, and he was. He got me one or two good parts.'

'He's got a lot of influence with Myers,' said Dick.

'He's acknowledged to be one of the best film editors and cutters in the place.'

'He may be all that, but I think he's horrible,' said Mary.

'He's like a great many of the men round here — or anywhere else for that matter,' said Dick. 'He takes advantage of his position.' He finished his coffee and pushed aside the empty cup. 'What are you girls going to do now?' he asked.

Irene shrugged her shapely shoulders.

'I'm going over to see Landser at R.L.A.,' she said. 'They're casting for a new picture and he promised me if there was anything going he would try to get me in.'

'I'm not doing anything until this afternoon,' said Mary. 'Why?'

'I feel like a walk,' replied Dick, 'and I hate walking alone.'

'I'll come with you,' said the girl. 'I feel like a walk too.'

'Go on, then, you two.' Irene searched in her bag for a cigarette. 'I'll stop here for a minute or two, I think.'

Dick rose and called the waitress. His forlorn hope that he might get Mary to himself had come off and he was feeling stupidly elated. He paid the small bill and left the little restaurant with Mary. They negotiated several small streets, chattering about everything and nothing, and presently came out on the Sunset Boulevard, the most wonderful street in the world. A distinguished-looking man who was strolling along towards them glanced twice at Mary, and even after he had passed took the trouble to look back. Mr. Thomas Spearman had an eye for beauty, particularly when it was feminine beauty, and the girl's face and figure pleased him. Quite three minutes after she had passed out of sight he speculated as to who she was, and then reverted to the thoughts that her appearance had interrupted.

There is no woman living who does not know when she has made an impression on a man, and very few to whom the knowledge fails to impart a pleasant sense of conquest. Mary Henley was no exception, and she mentally noted the admiring glance of the good-looking stranger and was secretly pleased. Dick had noticed it too.

'Who was that fellow?' he asked.

The girl shook her head. She'd been wondering that herself.

'I don't know,' she said. 'I've never seen him before.'

'He stared hard enough,' said Dick. 'I thought he knew you.'

'I think he'd like to know me,' said Mary calmly, 'but at the present moment we are not acquainted.'

Dick changed the subject, and in the interest of the ensuing conversation — a conversation that need not be recorded, since it was entirely of a personal nature — Mr. Spearman was forgotten.

And yet that chance meeting by two people entirely unknown to each other was to have an effect on both their lives. For in that momentary intermingling of glances something had been born which was to justify Mr. Spearman's existence and raise him into the sphere of the immortals.

Dick Rennit left Mary Henley at three o'clock and walked back to his small hotel treading on air. During that stroll with the girl he had succeeded in putting into words a great deal that had been locked up in his mind for the past three months, and he had found a willing — almost an eager — listener. That she had listened at all had given him cause for wonderment, but that she should have reciprocated by doing a little pleasant talking on her own account filled him with surprised ecstasy. The clear air of California seemed clearer; the sunshine more potent, the surroundings more lovely on account of those few words the girl had so softly and shyly uttered. Dick was hurrying along lost in speculations regarding the future, so oblivious to his immediate surroundings that he bumped into the man who was coming in the opposite direction.

'Say, what the hell's the matter with you?' grunted a voice angrily, and Dick was jerked back to the present.

'I'm sorry,' he stammered feebly, for the impact had winded him. 'I'm awfully — Why, it's Lamont!'

Perry Lamont glared at him.

'Why don't you look where you're going?' he demanded.

'I was thinking about something else,' said Dick. 'I hope I didn't hurt you.'

'You've given me an infernal kick on the shin,' grumbled the other, and then as Dick apologised and would have continued on his way: 'Don't go, Rennit; you're just the guy I'm looking for.'

'What is it?' said Dick. 'Have you got a job for me?'

Lamont's dark foreign-looking face broke into a smile — a peculiar smile that was not altogether pleasant. 'I may have — if you're sensible,' he replied meaningfully. 'Let's walk a bit.'

He took the younger man's arm, and Dick in frowning astonishment waited for what was corning next.

'I like you, Rennit,' went on Lamont, 'and I might be able to put something good in your way — if you're willing to do a little favour for me.'

His manner was graciousness itself, and Dick, who knew his man rather well, shot him a suspicious glance.

'It all depends about the favour,' he replied rather shortly.

'Quite an easy one,' said Lamont smoothly. 'You know that little blonde, Mary Henley?'

Dick felt the blood mounting to his face,

'Yes, I know her,' he said quietly. 'Why?'

'Well, I wish you'd get her to be a bit nicer to me,' said the other. 'I could do quite a lot for her if she'd treat me right, but the little fool's scared or something,'

Dick's mouth compressed, but he said nothing.

'The last time I saw her I asked her to come along to a bit of supper at my place,' said Lamont. 'She refused — quite angry about it she was too. Now you know her quite well, what about bringing her along tomorrow night? You could come with her and halfway through the supper have a telephone message or something calling you away.' He glanced at Dick with an ugly leer. 'What do you say about it?'

'I'll tell you,' said Dick hotly. 'I think you're a dirty swine!'

Lamont's dark eyes flashed.

'There's no need to get all lit up with cheap heroics,' he sneered. 'What are you making such a fuss for? I dare say the girl has been to any number of tête-à-tête supper parties — '

'That's a lie!' Dick's right arm shot out and his clenched fist thudded on the other's square jaw.

Lamont staggered, lost his balance, and fell sprawling on to the sidewalk. A little knot of passers-by who had seen the blow gathered round interestedly. Dick had acted in the heat of the moment, and now he felt a little ashamed of himself. Lamont, his face set in a scowl of fury, got slowly to his feet.

'I'll remember this, Rennit,' he breathed as he dusted himself down. 'I don't forget easily.'

'You can remember it as long as you like,' said Dick, 'and I'll give you something else to remember. Stop annoying Miss Henley, or the next time I shall do something worse than knocking you down.'

He turned on his heel and walked rapidly away. Lamont, with a furious glare at the people who had stopped, pushed his way angrily through them and stalked off in the opposite direction,

The small audience quickly broke up and went about their various businesses, quickly forgetting the incident. A week later, however, at least one of their number was to remember it very vividly indeed.

5

Introducing Mr. Paul Rivington

Nobody meeting Paul Rivington for the first time would ever have believed that he had once walked a beat as a uniformed policeman. Yet this was true, and his promotion had been amazingly rapid. Two years after he had first joined the Metropolitan Police Force he was a sergeant, and eighteen months after that had risen to an acting inspectorship in the C.I.D. He was liked by everybody, from the chief-commissioner to the youngest constable, and had been earmarked for further promotion, when, to the amazement of his superiors and friends, he had abruptly resigned. The excuse he gave was that he had taken up police work for a hobby, and that now he had acquired a sufficient knowledge of it he intended to devote himself to the examination of foreign police methods and the fascinating study of criminology.

He could afford to do this, for he had an income of six thousand a year, and was therefore not dependent on his pay or the pension which his resignation had lost him. He wanted more freedom than was possible under the administration at the Yard. As his own master he was able to undertake only that work which interested him. And it was not long before he had established a reputation for himself. Scotland Yard is a very jealous and a very loyal institution. It looks askance at the outsider and turns a freezing stare at the enthusiastic amateur.

But Paul Rivington had left the Yard with the good wishes of everyone, and was always ready to help the official police if he could. When Scotland Yard was at its wits' ends over the Danebridge murders he was called in by the assistant commissioner and worked with an official status. When he had justified this unusual procedure by bringing the case to a successful conclusion it had become quite a habit for headquarters to consult him in cases where especial difficulties confronted the patient investigators. Paul

Rivington was nearing fifty, a tall man with a clean-cut face that was rather stern except for the humorous twinkle in the grey eyes. His hair was dark and flecked with grey at the temples, and he was clean-shaven except for the tiny moustache which lay about the firm mouth, a smear of black over the tight, straight lips. He had never married, although at one period of his life he had vague ideas of doing so, and expended most of his affection on his younger brother.

Bob Rivington was fifteen years his junior, and as unlike him in outward appearance as it is possible for two men to be. Bob was short and inclined to stoutness, with a round, cheerful face and mouse-coloured hair. He was devoted to the elder man, and acted in the capacity of an unofficial secretary. They lived in a big house overlooking Hampstead Heath, a house that had been acquired by Paul Rivington's grandfather, and in which both he and his brother had been born.

For several days Paul had been a little irritable. Bob, who from long association knew his brother's every mood, did not have to look far for the reason. For the past month or so things had been very quiet. There was nothing in the newspapers of interest, and Paul, who liked nothing better than working at high pressure, had begun to weary of the inaction. Crime — or at least the kind of crime that interested him — seemed to have come to a sudden standstill. There were a few petty robberies and a smash-and-grab raid, but nothing that was not ordinary and commonplace. Bob was beginning to wonder how long this slump was going to last when he came back from a walk to find the whole atmosphere changed. His brother was seated at his desk busily writing, and about him was an air of alertness that was very different from the mood in which Bob had left him. He greeted his brother with a smile.

'How would you like a trip to Hollywood?' he asked, his eyes twinkling.

'Hollywood?' gasped Bob, taken completely by surprise.

Paul nodded.

'Hollywood, in California,' he explained, 'where the films are made, and most of the inhabitants apparently worship English policemen!'

Bob sat down a little hurriedly.

'I'd like it very much,' he replied. 'But why this sudden idea?'

His brother lit a cigarette and leaned back in his chair.

'Do you remember Elmer Myers?' he counter-questioned.

Bob wrinkled his forehead in thought.

'Elmer Myers?' he repeated. 'I seem to have heard the name, but I can't place it for the moment.'

'Elmer Myers came over here for a holiday two years ago, and got into the hands of Harvey, the con-man and his gang. They relieved him of fifty thousand pounds for a dud British picture company they said they were floating.'

'And you got it back.' His brother nodded quickly. 'Yes, I remember now. Rather a nice fellow, scared stiff that the business would get in the papers and everybody would laugh at him.'

'That's the man,' said Paul Rivington, drawing steadily at his cigarette, and blowing a wreath of smoke towards the ceiling. 'He came to me instead of going to the police so as to avoid publicity.' He paused, and Bob, impatient to hear the reason for the proposed trip, prompted him.

'Well,' he said, 'what has Elmer Myers got to do with this trip to Hollywood?'

'Everything,' answered Paul. 'He has inspired it.' He swung half round in his chair, so that he was completely facing the other. 'Just after you went out,' he went on, 'I had a transatlantic telephone call from Myers. He's in a frantic state, and wants me to go out at once.'

Bob's eyes sparkled.

'What's wrong?' he asked.

'Apparently he's just finished a super-picture — a sort of super-picture to end super-picture idea. He was full of superlatives about it — it cost a million dollars — never been anything like it in the history of the film industry, and all that. Well, the negative of this colossal masterpiece has been stolen, and Myers's film-editor and cutter, a fellow called Perry Lamont, murdered.'

Bob whistled.

'Sounds interesting,' he remarked.

'I thought so, too,' agreed his brother. 'That's why I booked a suite on the *Ile de France*, which leaves Southampton tomorrow morning.'

'Why didn't Myers get on to the Californian police? It would have saved time,' said Bob.

'I suggested that,' replied Paul, 'and his reason is that the theft of this film has got to be kept a secret. Mammoth Pictures haven't been doing so well lately, and this picture was to be their *magnum opus* and put them on their feet. Myers has borrowed money from the banks to make it, and he daren't apparently let them know that the thing's been stolen, or they'll all come down on him for the immediate return of their money, with the result that he'll have to go bankrupt.'

'I see,' said his brother. 'He wants you to get it back before anyone knows that it's been stolen?'

'That's the idea in a nutshell,' agreed Paul.

'It's going to be a pretty difficult job,' said Bob. 'By the time we get there the trail will be cold.'

'Icy,' said his brother with a shrug of his shoulders. 'I told Myers, but he begged me to come all the same; and anyway we can do our best.'

He rose to his feet and began to pace up and down.

'I must confess I'm terribly interested, because I think this is the first thing of its kind that's ever happened. It's entirely without precedent. A good many things have been stolen but never the negative of a super-picture before.'

'It sounds quite unique,' agreed Bob. 'Of course, without the negative they're helpless.'

'Oh, completely,' said his brother. 'The film might just as well never have been made. Unless it can be found, the only thing they could do would be to take the picture all over again, and that, from the expense point of view, is impossible.'

'Has Myers any suspicion who the people are that pinched it?' asked Bob.

Paul stopped in his walk, and nodded.

'I believe he has,' he replied. 'He hinted as much, but he wouldn't mention any names on the telephone.'

'If he's right, that's going to make the job a little easier,' said his brother.

Paul pursed his lips.

'There's a tremendous gulf between suspicion and certainty,' he said, 'and a larger one between certainty and proof. However, at the present moment I've only the vaguest details of the affair, so I think we will leave all speculation and discussion until after we have reached Hollywood and have seen Myers.'

6

The Double-Cross

Mr. Oscar Levenstein sat at his big desk, a scowl on his face and the end of a gold toothpick leaping up and down between his over-red lips. The presence of the toothpick was a sure sign that Mr. Levenstein was worried. The hour was very late; in fact, with the exception of Mr. Levenstein, the entire household had been in bed for over two hours. From time to time as he sat staring at the white blotting pad in front of him the film magnate shifted his gaze from the face of the little desk clock, and on these occasions his frown would deepen. He would raise his eyes from the clock to the open French windows, as though he were expecting somebody. He was in truth expecting Mr. Lefty Guinan and his satellite Spike Munro, and both these enterprising gentlemen were an hour late.

Mr. Levenstein's anger was slowly rising. He was not accustomed to people being late when he commanded their presence, for in his own sphere he was treated like a tin god, and the experience had rather spoiled him. The only evidence of his anger, however, lay in the erratic movement of the toothpick, for Mr. Levenstein had schooled himself never to show his emotion.

For another half-hour he sat there, and then a sound outside made him look towards the open windows, his head slightly on one side in a listening attitude. It was only a slight sound — the soft crunch of a foot on gravel, but it was the sound for which Mr. Levenstein had been waiting. He watched the blue oblong of the window, and presently a man's figure appeared against the moonlight and stepped into the room.

'You're late,' grunted Mr. Levenstein, and waved towards a chair.

Lefty Guinan came further into the room, and behind him appeared the smaller figure of Spike Munro

'Sure I'm late,' said Guinan, sitting

down. 'Couldn't get here before.'

It was significant that he made no form of apology. Mr. Levenstein noticed this and his eyes narrowed, but he made no comment. All he said was:

'What about this film? Have you brought it?'

Lefty Guinan leaned back in his chair and crossed his legs and shook his head.

'No,' he replied slowly. 'I guess I want to talk to you about that.'

Mr. Levenstein leaned forward and applied the end of his cigar to a desk-lighter.

'What is there to talk about?' he said. 'You've done your job, and I'm only waiting for you to hand over the picture before giving you the balance of the money.'

'That's what I want to talk about,' said Lefty Guinan smoothly.

'Well?' A harsh note had come into Mr. Levenstein's voice. 'It's waiting for you — twenty-five thousand dollars — in cash.'

'I've been kinder talkin' things over with Spike — ' Lefty jerked his head towards his silent companion. ' — and we've decided that twenty-five thousand bucks ain't enough.'

Mr. Munro, chewing steadily, bowed his head in confirmation. The man behind the desk looked from one to the other. Whatever he may have been thinking was impossible to judge from his expression.

'I see,' he said after a slight pause. 'You've decided it's not enough, eh?'

'Sure I have,' answered Guinan. 'The job was more difficult than I expected, and it's become much more dangerous — for us. The bumpin' off of that fellow Lamont would probably mean the chair for us if we were caught. I guess it wouldn't be any good us swearin' we had nothin' to do with it; nobody 'ud believe us.'

'I don't suppose they would,' said Mr. Levenstein dryly. 'I'm not sure that I believe you myself.'

'That don't worry me any,' retorted Guinan. 'I've told you the truth; the fellow was dead when we got there — '

'Never mind about that,' broke in Levenstein impatiently. 'I'm not the least interested in Perry Lamont, alive or dead. You're not satisfied with the amount that we agreed on? How much more do you want?'

'Two hundred thousand dollars,' said Lefty Guinan briefly.

'That,' said Mr. Levenstein, 'is absurd. 'Talk sense!'

'Sure, I am talkin' sense,' said Guinan. 'There's a lot of sense in two hundred thousand dollars.'

'Supposing I refuse to pay that amount,' said Oscar Levenstein. 'What happens then?'

Lefty uncrossed his legs and sat forward.

'Well, then,' he said, 'I guess we don't part with that film.'

There was a short silence. Mr. Munro's jaws continued to move up and down rhythmically. Mr. Levenstein steadily drew on his cigar, blowing a series of smoke rings towards the ceiling.

'If you keep the film,' he said, at last, 'you get nothing more from me. The film is of no value to you at all — '

'Sure it isn't, but it's of value to

Mammoth Pictures,' interrupted Lefty Guinan. 'Maybe if you won't pay up they'll be only too glad to hand over what I've asked to get it back.'

For a second Mr. Levenstein's face was distorted by a spasm of rage, and it looked so threatening that Lefty Guinan's hand went to his hip pocket. Before he could pull the gun, however, the mask had dropped again and the film magnate's face was expressionless.

'So that's the idea, is it?' he said smoothly. 'A little double-crossing, eh? My friend, let me tell you that Mammoth Pictures hasn't got two hundred thousand cents, let alone dollars.'

'I guess they'd find them quick enough,' said Guinan. 'They've got to have that film back to save themselves from ruin. Yes, sir, they'd sure find the cash quick enough, and gladly.'

There was another pause while Mr. Levenstein thoughtfully examined the glowing end of his cigar.

'Supposing,' he said presently, 'I agree to your terms. When do I get the film?'

'Tomorrow mornin',' answered Lefty

promptly. 'Make a date and I'll hand over the film in exchange for the cash.'

'Very well.' Mr. Levertstein nodded. 'I agree. Meet me at the disused studio at ten-thirty, bring the film, and I'll bring the cash.'

'Sure that's a deal.' Lefty rose to his feet. 'I'll be there sharp on time.'

He held out his hand, but Mr. Levenstein suddenly became short-sighted.

'Good night,' he said briefly, and nodded towards the French windows.

On the way back to their lodgings Lefty became voluble concerning his cleverness.

'Didn't I tell you it would work all right?' he chuckled delightedly. 'Two hundred thousand bucks as easy as kiss your hand! And if I hadn't been smart we might have put up with a mouldy twenty-five thousand.'

'Sure you're a swell guy,' said sycophantic Mr. Munro.

'It was easier than I thought it would be,' said Lefty. 'I guess he saw that I meant what I said, and that it was no use arguin'. Spike, we'll open that bottle of hooch and celebrate.'

They reached their sitting-room at Mack's in high spirits, and as the rye whisky which Guinan produced from his suitcase fell lower in the bottle so their spirits rose correspondingly.

'Here's to the million-dollar film,' said Lefty a little thickly, raising his fifth glass and gulping the contents at a draught. 'Let's bring it out and have a look at it.'

He got up, took a key from his pocket and unlocked his big cabin trunk. From it he took a large circular steel box and carried it back to the table.

'Might as well look at it for the last time,' he said, jerking back the lid and displaying the rolls of celluloid. 'Take a look at that, Spike; that's the thing that's put two hundred thousand bucks in our pockets!'

He pulled out a big roll of film and held it up to the light.

'Sure, it's fine — ' began Spike, but his words were drowned in a howl of rage which burst from Lefty Guinan's lips.

'This ain't the film!' he cried. 'Look at this, Spike!'

He flung the reel across the room at his companion, half sobbing with disappointment and fury.

'That old devil's done us! He's done us! But I'll get even with him, the old — ! I'll kill him for this!' He stopped, panting, and Mr. Munro picked up the roll of film and looked at it.

It was a very worn copy of one of Charlie Chaplin's earlier comedies!

7

The Conference

Mr. Elmer Myers paced up and down the big study of his house at Beverley Hills. It was a comfortable room — the room of a worker. There were people who said that Mr. Myers' study was more like an office than a room in a private house, and to these the managing director of Mammoth Pictures would invariably reply:

'Well, I guess I do the greater part of my work here, so why shouldn't it be like an office?'

Neither Mr. Myers nor Frank Leyland, who stood staring out through the tall French windows on to the neatly shaven lawn, was working at that moment. The young film director looked harassed and worried; there were dark rings under his eyes and signs of strain round his mouth. Even in the middle of making a film, when he sometimes worked for sixteen hours at a stretch, he had never looked like this. As for Elmer Myers, no one would have recognised him as the big genial man of a fortnight ago. His clothes hung on him loosely, as though his body had wasted, and the skin of his face was flabby and unhealthy-looking. Great puffy pouches of leaden-coloured flesh underlined his eyes, and two deep creases had appeared between his brows, and his lips, once so firm, had become loose and moved constantly as though he were speaking to himself.

He came over to the chair behind the littered table, hesitated uncertainly, and dropped into it heavily.

'What are we going to do, Frank?' he said hopelessly.

Frank Leyland turned from his aimless and unprofitable contemplation of the garden and walked slowly to the desk. He wondered how many times Elmer Myers had made the same remark since the loss of the super-film and the murder of Lamont.

'What can we do,' he asked, perching himself on the edge of the big oak table, 'except wait for this fellow Rivington to arrive?'

'Nothing, I suppose.' Elmer Myers passed a hand that shook over his eyes. 'We can't afford delay, Frank; only this morning the renters rang up, asking when they could have a copy of the film so that they could arrange the trade show. I had to stall 'em, but I can't keep on stallin' 'em. Sooner or later, unless we can get the picture back, I'll have to tell 'em the truth, and then — ' He made an expressive gesture. 'The banks'll go up in the air and so shall I!'

'You've got a pretty good excuse at the moment,' said Leyland, 'in the fact that Lamont was killed. You can stick to your story that he and I were in the middle of cutting the picture. That's a good excuse for not having it ready.'

'I guess that's all right as far as it goes, Frank,' agreed Elmer Myers, 'but how far has it got to go? I can't keep it up forever. And there's no reason why we shouldn't get hold of another cutter.'

'The only thing we can do is to wait for Rivington and hope for the best,' said

Frank Leyland. He reached over and patted the older man on the shoulder. 'Cheer up, Elmer, perhaps something will happen to straighten things out.'

'You're a good guy, Frank,' said Mr. Myers, and there was a little catch in his voice. 'I don't know what I should have done without you. Gone clean crazy, I reckon. You're the only fellow I've been able to open up to and it's helped.'

'What are the police doing about Lamont's death?' asked the young director.

'That's one of the things that's worrying me,' confessed Elmer Myers. 'I saw Captain Willing this morning, and apparently they've got some idea that young Dick Rennit had something to do with it.'

'Rennit?' Leyland frowned for a second, and then his face cleared. 'You mean the stunt man?'

'That's the guy,' he answered. 'Apparently he had a quarrel with Lamont and knocked him down or something on Sunset Boulevard. Anyway, somebody has come forward and given information to that effect.'

'But it's a lot of rubbish!' exclaimed

Leyland. 'It's obvious that the people who got into the studio that night were experts, and that there were two of them. What about the watchman's story and the way the doors were opened? They used a blowpipe. It's absurd to suspect Rennit.'

'Sure, that's what I said,' answered Myers, 'but I don't think the argument cut any ice with Willing. His idea is that Rennit was in with this bunch of crooks. He got them to break into the studios, and finding Lamont there, took the opportunity to pay off a little private score of his own.'

'What was the cause of the quarrel between Lamont and Rennit?' asked Leyland.

'It was over some girl or other,' said Myers. 'You know what Lamont was like. I guess he was a good cutter, but his goodness finished there! The thing is, Frank, that if they arrest Rennit I'm going to be in a pretty bad position.'

'How?' said the other.

'Why, don't you see I shall have to let out about the picture,' answered Myers. 'At the present moment they don't know anything about that. I've kept it under my hat. When they asked me I told them nothing had been stolen, and if they arrest this guy I shall have to speak.'

Frank Leyland nodded slowly, and the worried look on his good-looking face deepened.

'I suppose you will,' he said softly. 'Yes, of course you will.'

There was a moment's silence.

'Rennit couldn't have had anything to do with the stealing of the film, could he?' he asked presently.

Elmer Myers pursed up his lips.

'I shouldn't think so,' he said, shaking his head. 'I guess the only man who had anything to do with that is Levenstein.'

'But Levenstein didn't do it himself,' retorted the young director. 'It was probably his scheme, but he must have hired somebody to carry it out, and why shouldn't that have been Rennit?'

Mr. Myers's eyebrows descended until they stretched in a straight line across his forehead.

'There may be something in that,' he admitted. 'Rennit's done a whole lot of

76

work for World Wide Films, and knows Levenstein well. Yes, I guess there might be something in that, Frank.'

'It isn't going to help much, anyway,' said Leyland gloomily. 'You know, Elmer, the thing that's worrying me is that the negative may have been destroyed.'

'That's what's worrying me,' said the managing director of Mammoth Pictures, 'and if it's got to Levenstein's hands I guess that's what happened. And if that's the case, I'm sunk.'

He stared at the mass of untidy papers before him, a rather pathetic figure. Frank Leyland, who genuinely liked this man, experienced a wave of sympathy for him. Slipping down from his seat on the edge of the big table, he walked round and dropped his hand lightly on the hunched shoulders.

'Let's try and be optimistic, Elmer,' he said, forcing his voice to a cheery note he was far from feeling. 'Perhaps it's not as bad as all that — '

He looked up quickly as a shadow darkened the window. Mr. Myers looked up too.

'Who the hell — ' he began, and then the tall man who had paused outside crossed the threshold.

'Mr. Myers?' he said pleasantly. 'You must forgive my unceremonious method of entering your house, but in the circumstances it was the only way.'

Mr. Myers rose quickly and stood, his hands gripping the edge of the writing-table while he stared at the newcomer. And then to his tired eyes came recognition.

'By gosh, it's Rivington!' he cried, and the next moment was round the desk, gripping the other's hand and shaking it warmly.

Paul smiled. 'This — ' He turned to Bob who had followed him through the window. ' — is my brother; I think you met him when you were over in England. If Bob and I could have a wash and a drink — '

'OK,' said Elmer Myers. 'Come with me, and I'll take you up to the bathroom. Wait here, will you, Frank; we shan't be long.'

Leyland nodded, and crossing to the

door, Mr. Myers held it open for his unexpected guests. Frank Leyland waited impatiently for them to return.

Three minutes later, feeling — and looking — a great deal better for their wash, Paul and Bob settled themselves in the comfortable chairs which Elmer Myers pushed forward. With stiff drinks before them, they listened to their host's account of the robbery of the film and his suspicions of Levenstein's part in it.

'You see the position now,' said Mr. Myers, when he had finished, 'and I guess it's a darned unpleasant one.'

'It is,' said Paul sympathetically. 'Of course, this man Levenstein was counting on the fact that you would have, for your own sake, to keep quiet about the film having been stolen. He hoped that it would prevent you calling in the police, in case the secret should leak out.'

'He knows that I dare not let it become known until I'm absolutely forced to,' said Elmer Myers. 'And I suppose he thought by that time he would have succeeded in covering up his tracks. Now, Rivington, you know all about it. Do you think there's any chance of your being able to help?'

Paul looked at the drawn, anxious face of the man before him, and his heart was full of anger at the meanness of the plot that had been hatched against him.

'If that negative is still in existence,' he said, 'I'll get it back for you.'

Elmer Myers stretched out a hand.

'Thank you,' he said simply.

8

Exit Mr. Levenstein

The discovery that the film on which he had banked so much was gone filled Lefty Guinan's heart with a bitter and consuming rage. He stamped up and down his room, uttering the most lurid oaths and curses, and heedless of the pacific attempts of Spike Munro to quieten him down.

'There ain't no sense going ga-ga,' said Mr. Munro, helping himself to a fresh wad of gum and munching it steadily. 'What we've gotta do is to look at the thing calmly.'

It was excellent advice, and ordinarily Mr. Guinan would have been the first to admit it, but his temper had got the better of him and he was impervious to reason.

'Look at it calmly!' he cried savagely. 'Sure, that's right, take it as a joke! We've lost two hundred and twenty-five thousand dollars, and that old devil is laughing at us up his sleeve!'

'You ain't sure he took the film,' replied Spike. 'I guess I don't see how he could. There wasn't time.'

'What do you mean, there wasn't time?' snarled Mr. Guinan. 'There was whales of time.'

'How could he have got here and got away again after we left him?' began Spike argumentatively. 'It ain't possible!'

'Ain't you got brains?' snapped Lefty. 'I'm not sayin' he pinched the thing tonight. There were other times he could have done it, wasn't there? We haven't looked at the thing for three days until just now.'

'There's something in that,' said Spike, partly convinced.

'There's a lot in that,' retorted Lefty. 'No wonder the old devil agreed to part so easily. I guess he knew he'd never have to pay out his money, the mean old skinflint. But I'll get him, I'll show him that he can't double-cross me.'

He began putting on his overcoat.

'What are you going to do?' asked Spike.

'I'm going up to Levenstein's and have

it out with him,' replied Guinan. 'I guess he can do what he likes with the film, but I'm going to have that money.'

The usual taciturn and sycophantic Mr. Munro put his foot down.

'Don't be a fool, Lefty,' he said. 'Levenstein's probably gone to bed, and, anyway, you're not in a fit state to see him tonight. You're all lit up with hooch.'

Lefty Guinan glared at his companion; he was not used to being spoken to in that way, particularly by the easygoing Spike.

'Say, cut that out!' he murmured thickly. 'I'm going to have it out with that old twister.'

'I'm in this as well as you, ain't I?' said Spike Munro firmly. 'And if you do anythin' silly I'm goin' to get it in the neck as well as you. What's the sense in goin' all the way to Levenstein's house when you're goin' to see him in the mornin'?'

'If he turns up,' growled Lefty.

'Sure he'll turn up,' answered Spike. 'I guess that if he's pinched that film he's not going to admit the fact by not turnin'' up. He'll turn up and he'll bring the money with him, and that'll be our chance to get him. It'll be easy enough at that place to do anythin' and get away with it.'

The angry glare died out of Lefty Guinan's eyes and he slowly took off his overcoat.

'I guess you're right, Spike,' he said grudgingly. 'Sure we can make the old beggar part up at that place, and, by heck, we will!' He clenched his fist and brought it down with a smash on the table. 'We'll beat him up so that his own mother wouldn't know him — if he ever had one!'

Mr. Munro chewed steadily and silently. He had achieved his object and was not given to wasting words. They went to bed at last, and the rye whisky they had drunk brought a heavy and dreamless sleep.

When he awoke in the morning, however, Lefty Guinan's anger had in no way abated; if anything, it had increased. His rather blustering rage of the previous night had been replaced by a cold and infinitely more dangerous state of mind.

When he and Spike set out for the disused studios where it had been arranged they should meet Mr. Oscar Levenstein there was murder in his heart.

They were ten minutes early, but they found the fat little film magnate waiting for them outside the big gate.

'I couldn't get in,' he said shortly. 'You've got the only key.'

Lefty grunted. He couldn't trust himself to speak casually, and what he had to say he wanted to reserve until they were inside. He unlocked the small wicket gate that was set in the larger one, and stepped through into the untidy courtyard. Spike and Mr. Levenstein followed him.

'Now,' said Mr. Levenstein impatiently when Guinan had closed the little gate. 'I don't want to hang about here longer than I can help — where's that film?'

Lefty Guinan faced him and his expression was ugly.

'I guess you should know that,' he snarled meaningfully.

Mr. Levenstein's hairless brows shot upwards.

'I don't get you,' he said coldly. 'The arrangement was that you were to bring the film here at ten o'clock this morning and that in exchange for it I was to hand you over two hundred and twenty-five thousand dollars.'

'I guess I know the arrangement all right,' snapped Guinan. 'Sure, it was a clever arrangement, wasn't it? You thought you were being very smart, didn't you?'

'I don't know what you're talking about,' said Oscar Levenstein angrily.

'I'll say you don't!' sneered Lefty Guinan. 'Sure, you don't. You don't know anythin' about that film, do you?'

'I only know that you should have brought it here as you promised,' said the other, and his eyes narrowed. 'What's the idea of all this? If you've got it into your head that you can squeeze me for some more money you're mistaken. I agreed to your demand for an extra two hundred thousand dollars, but I'll see you in hell before you get another cent.'

'I guess you do it fine and dandy.' Lefty Guinan nodded in mock admiration. 'But it don't cut any ice with this baby!'

'You're talking in riddles,' grunted the magnate.

'Am I?' Guinan thrust his face forward until it was only a few inches from Mr. Levenstein's. 'Well, I guess I'll speak plainer, you double-crossing swine! You know very well that we can't hand over that film, because we haven't got it to hand over.'

He spat the words out viciously, and Mr. Levenstein, a little alarmed, took a step backwards.

'What do you mean you haven't got it — ' he began, when the full force of Lefty Guinan's pent-up fury broke.

'Ain't I speakin' plainly?' he hissed. 'An' you can stop bluffin', Levenstein, as quickly as you like. It doesn't get across. We know you pinched that film and that you've got it — '

'I've got it?' Oscar Levenstein's brows drew together in a frown. 'Don't talk rubbish. How could I have got it?'

'The same way as we got it,' retorted Guinan. 'You pinched it from the trunk in my room and left an old comedy of Chaplin's in its place. I guess you thought we shouldn't know who'd taken it, but we're not such saps as all that, and if you think you're goin' to get away with it, you're not. You don't leave this place until you've handed over the cash, so you can make up your mind to that!'

As if by magic an ugly blue-nosed automatic had suddenly appeared in his hand, its menacing muzzle covering the fat body of the film magnate. Mr. Levenstein's large face went a dirty grey.

'Put that thing away,' he cried hastily. 'All this stuff you're telling me is bunk. I don't know anything about the film except that you're supposed to bring it here this morning, and if somebody's stolen it, it wasn't me.'

'Sure, it wasn't!' said Lefty Guinan, and his eyes were murderous. 'I guess nobody else knew it was there. You can't get away with it, Levenstein. You've got that picture and you've got to pay up as agreed.'

'I see.' Oscar Levenstein's thin lips curled back, showing his white teeth in an unpleasant sneer. 'You want jam on the gingerbread. So this is the new idea, eh?

You tried blackmail, and now you're going to try a hold-up. You want to get two hundred and twenty-five thousand dollars out of me and then you'll go and take that negative back to Mammoth Pictures. It's a swell idea, but I reckon it ain't coming off. You can go to hell!'

'Can I?' Lefty Guinan's face became convulsed with sudden fury. 'Well see who'll reach there first.'

His fingers tightened on the trigger of the automatic, and from the black muzzle came a stream of death. Mr. Levenstein's fat body gave a convulsive start as the bullets tore their way into his flesh. For a moment he stood rigid, staring at the gangster with a ludicrous expression of surprise, and then he seemed to crumple up, and without a cry fell, an obese, sprawling figure, on the concrete court-yard.

'My God, what have you done, Lefty?' whispered Spike hoarsely, and there was horror in his voice.

'Can it!' snarled Guinan, and his face had gone the colour of chalk. He was gazing at the still figure of the man he had killed as if it had been a ghost. 'I didn't mean to do it. I guess I lost my temper — '

'Let's get away!' whined the frightened Mr. Munro. 'It's a chair job now, if we're caught.'

With an effort his companion pulled himself together and thrust the still smoking pistol into his pocket.

'We're not goin' to be caught,' he said, 'but we're not goin' empty-handed. This guy's got a wad of bucks on him which belongs to us, and we're goin' to have it.'

He bent swiftly over the body of the film magnate, and presently straightened up holding a thick roll of bills.

'Now let's move,' he said, and went over to the wicket gate.

Drawn up close against the wall was an expensive-looking coupé, and Lefty climbed up into the driver's seat and pressed the starter. The engine started up at once, and almost before Spike had succeeded in scrambling in beside him Lefty had let in the clutch and sent the car jerking forward. He found some difficulty in turning the machine round in the narrow confines of the road, but he managed it. With ever-increasing speed the car shot down the road, negotiating a series of secondary roads, and came out into the main boulevard. But Lefty did not keep to this very long. A mile farther on he turned into a side street and passed a scattering of small houses into a stretch of road that ran along the foot of the hill. Here he brought the car to a halt and got out.

'We'll leave the thing here,' he said to Spike, looking quickly round to make sure there was nobody in sight, 'and get back to Mack's on foot. After that we'll pay the score and clear off back to Chicago as quickly as we can.' He patted his hip pocket, and his unpleasant face broke into a smile. 'And we're not goin' empty-handed, boy,' he added. 'We've got a pile that'll help us to hit the high-spots!'

They reached the hotel-restaurant, and while Spike hastily packed their belongings Lefty sought out the proprietor and paid their bill, making an excuse for their hasty departure that sounded fairly probable. Then he went over to the filling station to get the car he had bought, and here he got a shock. A tall, well-dressed man was talking to the clerk in charge, and as Mr. Guinan approached he turned and they met almost face to face.

'Well, if it isn't Lefty,' drawled Mr. Spearman, with just the right amount of surprise in his voice. 'What are you doing in Hollywood, Lefty? Going to be a film star?'

9

Lefty Guinan Does a Little Thinking

Lefty Guinan eyed the good-looking Mr. Spearman suspiciously.

'What are you doing here?' he asked.

'Having a holiday,' said Mr. Spearman, waving his hand. 'Just living a life of leisure!'

'At whose expense?' granted Lefty, who had no illusions concerning the man he was speaking to. 'Who's the sucker?'

Mr. Spearman looked pained.

'Don't be offensive, Lefty,' he chided gently. 'There's no sucker — what a vulgar word that is. I've gone into business.'

Guinan smiled unpleasantly.

'Whose business?' he asked. 'And how did you get in? With a jemmy?'

'Captain Chase' looked round cautiously. The filling station clerk had moved away and was attending to another customer

93

well out of earshot.

'You ask too many questions,' he replied. 'You're full of questions, Lefty, but if you must know I'm in the film business.'

'I see.' Mr. Guinan's unpleasant smile changed to a sneer. 'In the film business, eh? What are you — cameraman, director, or star?'

'I think you might describe me as an impresario,' said Tommy Spearman guardedly. 'You don't know what that means, but it's a very good description.'

'Suppose you quit telling fairy tales and come down to facts,' growled Lefty Guinan. 'First you say you're havin' a holiday, then you tell me you've gone into business. What are you really doing?'

'Is there any real reason why I should tell you that?' said the other with a beaming smile. 'Is it anything to do with you?'

'I guess I'm naturally interested in an old friend,' said Lefty, and Mr. Spearman shook his head.

'I'm no friend of yours, Lefty,' he said. 'An acquaintance, perhaps, but not a friend.'

He laughed, and Guinan wondered what was amusing him.

'We met once or twice in Chicago, but we never became what you might call bosom pals. By the way, how's Spike? Still chewing himself to death?'

'He's OK, so far as I know,' said Lefty Guinan hastily. 'I haven't seen him for weeks — '

'Dear me, is that so?' Mr. Spearman's eyes went up in amazement. 'What a long time it must have taken you to walk across from Mack's.'

'What do you mean?' demanded Lefty.

'I saw you and Spike go into Mack's an hour ago,' said Mr. Spearman gently. 'What are you boys doing in Hollywood — having a good time?'

Lefty Guinan was silent. He had hoped that Tommy Spearman would be ignorant of the fact that Spike Munro was with him, for it was a well-known fact that when they were together there was business afoot.

'They tell me,' Mr. Spearman went on, looking at him quizzically, 'that you're in the film trade, too.'

Lefty started, and his small eyes became slits.

'Who told you?' he demanded loudly. 'I'm in the film trade? What do I know about films?'

'I never thought you knew anything,' said Mr. Spearman. 'I don't suppose you could tell a two-reel comedy from a super-picture, could you, Lefty?'

'Say, what are you getting at?' said Lefty Guinan suspiciously. 'What's all this talk about films?'

'What else can you talk about in Hollywood?' said Mr. Spearman innocently. 'Everybody talks about films in this city, Lefty. If you don't talk about films here you might just as well have been born dumb. Why shouldn't they talk about films? Look at the money they've made out of them. There's that fellow, Levenstein — somebody pointed him out to me yesterday, he's a millionaire several times over, and all his money was made out of films.'

Lefty Guinan felt the colour leave his face.

'I don't know anything about this

what's-his-name Levenstein,' he said quickly, 'and I don't know anything about films. Spike and I just came here for a bit of a rest and a look round. We're going back to Chicago today.'

'Feeling all the better for your rest, I hope,' said Spearman politely. 'It must have cost you a bit, Lefty; you've been spending money pretty freely while you've been here.'

'You seem to know a lot about me,' growled Lefty a little uncomfortably. 'Takin' a mighty big interest in my business, ain't you?'

'I'm interested in everybody's business but my own,' confessed Mr. Spearman. 'I'm built that way. Everything interests me — even that murder at Mammoth Pictures' place. You've no idea how interested I was in that. Were you interested too?'

'Sure,' said Guinan. 'I heard about it, of course, but I guess I'm not fond of murders.'

'Who is?' said Mr. Spearman. 'Well, let's stop talking shop. So you've finished your holiday and you're going back to

Chicago, are you? Taking anything with you?'

'Say, what should I be taking?' demanded Lefty violently. He was feeling more than a little uneasy. There was a hidden meaning behind Mr. Spearman's words that he did not like at all. This cool, well-dressed man knew something, and Lefty Guinan was not quite sure how much.

'A picture postcard or two of Hollywood, or some little souvenir of your visit,' said Mr. Spearman. 'But perhaps you don't like souvenirs? Well, some of them can be very unpleasant.'

He smiled broadly and turned away.

'I must be going, Lefty. I've got my film business to look after. Perhaps I'll see you sometime. Give my love to Spike, and tell him to cut out the gum habit. Vice in any form is revolting.'

He waved his hand and walked away, leaving Lefty Guinan to make his arrangements for his car in a very thoughtful mood. When he got back to Mack's he found Mr. Munro waiting impatiently.

'You've been a long time,' he greeted. 'I was wondering what had happened.'

Lefty Guinan poured out himself a drink and gulped it down.

'Say, who do you think I met at the filling station,' he said.

'I guess I'm not good at riddles,' grunted Spike. 'Go easy with that stuff. It's all we've got, and I'd like some. Who did you see?'

'Tommy Spearman,' said Lefty, splashing some whisky into Spike's glass.

'Is that guy here?' said Mr. Munro. 'I thought Hollywood was select!'

'Sure he's here,' Lefty nodded. 'Very much here. He was talking a lot of stuff that I can't get the hang of.'

'What do you mean?' Mr. Munro drank half his drink and began to unwrap a new packet of gum. 'What sort of stuff?'

'It may be a lot of bunk, and it may not,' said Lefty Guinan, lighting a cigarette. 'But he seems to know a lot too much for my liking.'

'About what?' asked Spike sharply.

'About us,' answered Guinan.

'Why — what did he say?' the little

man's voice was anxious.

'I guess it wasn't so much what he actually said,' replied Lefty thoughtfully, blowing a stream of smoke towards the ceiling. 'It was what he hinted.'

So far as he could remember he repeated his conversation with Mr. Spearman.

'I don't like it,' said Spike, shaking his head. 'That fellow's hot! He's so hot that when he sits down at the table all the butter melts! It looks to me as though he knows what we've been doing.'

'Sure, that's what I think,' agreed Guinan, 'and I was wondering what he knows.'

'Lots of people have wondered that,' answered Spike. 'Look at Lew Conner. He and his boys planned a bust on the Chicago Federal Bank and got away with ten thousand bucks. The night after Mr. bloomin' Spearman lifted the lot, though nobody knew how he knew anything about it. Conner was like a ragin' bull for weeks — '

Lefty Guinan uttered an exclamation and his face set.

'Sure, Spike, you've hit it!' he exclaimed. 'That's where the film went to!'

'Eh?' Mr. Munro looked up, startled at the vehemence of his companion.

'Spearman pinched it!' cried Lefty excitedly. 'I guess that's what he meant by going into the film business and all that guff. It wasn't Levenstein at all — it was Spearman.'

Spike Munro frowned and slipped the chunk of chewing gum he had been extracting from its wrappings into his mouth.

'It's just the sort of thing he would do,' he said. 'I wish I'd thought of that while I was talkin' to him,' snarled Lefty, his face dark with anger. 'But I'll bet I'm right. He must have been spyin' on us and found out. The dirty crook, I'd like — '

'Why get all lit up?' said Mr. Munro calmly. 'What does it matter, anyhow? Let him keep the film; we've got the money, ain't we, and that's all that matters.'

'Sure, we've got the money all right,' said Lefty.

'Talkin' of money,' said Mr. Munro cautiously, 'what about sharin' out now? You never know what might happen; we might have to separate or anythin'.'

'All right, I'll divide up,' said Guinan,

but his voice did not sound too eager. 'Two-thirds to me, and a third to you — '

'Fifty-fifty,' broke in Mr. Munro gently. 'Fifty-fifty, Lefty. Don't you go tryin' no funny stuff.'

'Two-thirds was what we agreed,' began Lefty argumentatively, and put his hand in his breast pocket where he had put the roll of bills he had taken from the dead body of the unfortunate Levenstein. 'I guess I planned the whole business, didn't I?' He broke off and his jaw dropped. 'It's gone!' he shouted. 'I put it in my pocket, and it's gone!'

Mr, Munro stopped in the middle of chewing, and his thin face looked very unpleasant.

'Say, don't try and work that old stuff on me, Lefty,' he said angrily. 'I heard that gag when I was a baby.'

'Don't be a fool!' cried Lefty Guinan, frantically searching his pockets. 'I'm not trying to work any gag on you. The money's gone, I tell you!'

The light of understanding came into Spike's eyes.

'Did you have it with you when you

were talking to Tommy Spearman?' he asked.

'Sure, I did,' snapped Lefty. 'In my breast pocket — '

'Then I guess it's in his pocket now,' said Spike. 'That fellow's the cleverest 'dip' that was ever born.'

Lefty Guinan's face was not pretty as he looked at his companion. 'By the time I've finished with him,' he muttered harshly, 'he'll wish he never had been born!'

10

Mr. Spearman is Sympathetic

Mr. Thomas Spearman alias Captain Garvin Chase, left the filling station after his meeting with Lefty Guinan and walked happily along Sunset Boulevard to his lunch. He hummed a tune below his breath as he walked — a gay little tune that reflected the state of Mr. Spearman's mind. His morning's walk had been very profitable, and not before it was time, for his funds were getting very low indeed.

The two hundred and twenty-five thousand dollars that he had taken so dexterously from Lefty Guinan's pocket would prove very useful. He had never expected to reap such a harvest, and when he had taken the wallet he had taken it more for a joke than anything else. Well, it had proved a very good joke, and he wondered if Mr. Guinan was laughing, and smiled. He could picture the crook's face when he discovered his loss — and Spike Munro's. What a lot of chewing gum it would take to soften that disappointment.

He strolled on, basking in the sunshine and feeling at peace with the world. There was still the film deal to pull off, but now he could wait until the time was riper. The longer he kept it the more valuable it would become as a source of revenue, for it was his experience that the more anxious people got, the more they were prepared to pay to relieve their anxiety.

It had been his first intention to play Levenstein and Myers off against each other: the one who offered the most getting the film. But in the meanwhile he had made one or two inquiries, and the result had made him change his plan. In spite of the fact that his honesty would not bear a very close inspection, Mr. Spearman was something of a sentimentalist. Being a sentimentalist, his sympathies were with the underdog. He had no intention of handing the film back to Myers with his blessing, but he was determined that nobody else should be in the market for it.

He had planned the whole thing care-fully. That night he was sending Myers a neat little letter, telling him that if he was prepared to pay a hundred thousand dol-lars he could have the film back. Mr. Myers was to bring the money himself in dollar bills and stop his car halfway along Sunset Boulevard at two o'clock in the morning. At that hour the most beautiful thoroughfare in the world would be as still and empty as the Sahara desert. There he would be met, and in exchange for the money the film would be handed over.

If he brought anybody with him the deal would be off. Mr. Spearman, after much consideration, had decided that this was quite a good idea. He was not the least afraid that Myers would inform the police; he had learned enough at the interview he had overheard between Guinan and Levenstein to know that that was the last thing that Myers dare do.

He would be only too pleased at the chance of getting his picture back without any publicity to risk a hitch. The hundred thousand dollars was, Mr. Spearman concluded, already in his pocket, and added to what by a stroke of luck he had already, would represent quite a respectable sum.

His thoughts changed from such mundane things to the girl he had seen that day on Sunset Boulevard. He had seen her several times since, and almost felt that he knew her, although they had never spoken.

It was just about here that he had first met her, and experienced for the first time in his adventurous life an unaccountable quickening of the pulse. Twice after he had seen her with the same good-looking young fellow who had been with her that day, and once alone. On the last occasion he had almost spoken, and in passing she had half smiled, and then evidently remembering that he was a stranger, the smile had broken off short, to become replaced by a look of stony indifference.

Mr. Spearman sighed. He would have liked to have talked to that girl just for the pleasure of watching her smile — really smile. Well, it was very doubtful if he would ever do that, and it was pretty obvious that she was booked. Engaged to the fellow he had seen her with, perhaps, or married maybe.

On the third occasion he had seen her he had looked for the ring, but her hand had been gloved. He walked on, still thinking of the girl, and then as he reached the beginning of the Wilshire Boulevard and came in sight of his hotel he saw her.

She was walking slowly towards him. As she passed him he saw that her face was white and drawn, and with a little tug at his heart, that she had been crying. Acting on a sudden impulse, he swung round, and in four strides had reached her side.

'Excuse me,' he said diffidently, lifting his hat, 'is there anything the matter? You look — ill.'

Mary Henley stopped and raised her eyes. Her first inclination was to make a sharp retort and pass on. Then she saw who it was and the concern in his eyes.

'Thank you,' she said, and her voice shook in spite of all her efforts to keep it steady. 'I am — I am quite all right.'

'You look far from all right,' he answered gravely. 'You look really all in.

Won't you come along to the Beverley Wilshire and sit down for a few minutes?'

She hesitated.

'You're thinking that I'm trying to be fresh, aren't you?' he said quickly. 'But really I'm not I've seen you so often that although I don't know you I feel as if you were an old friend — if you can understand that.'

She could and did understand that. Strangely enough, she felt the same way about this man. He was not a stranger in the true sense of the word.

'I think it's terribly kind of you,' she said. 'I would like a rest for a moment. I — I've had rather a shock.'

'We'll have some coffee,' said Mr. Spearman. 'Everybody will be at lunch, and the lounge will be almost empty.'

'What about your lunch?' she asked as they turned and walked towards the Beverley Wilshire.

'I never eat lunch,' he said hastily and untruthfully.

She sank gratefully into one of the padded chairs with which the lounge was furnished and Mr. Spearman ordered coffee.

He gave her a cigarette, which she accepted, and when the waiter had brought the coffee and gone away, he said:

'Now you can talk or not, just as you like. I don't want to pry into your private affairs, but if I can do anything to help I'd be only too pleased.'

She shook her head.

'I'm afraid you couldn't do anything,' she said, and was silent for such a long time that Mr. Spearman was beginning to fear that he had offended her.

He had just opened his mouth to apologise, when she spoke.

'I may as well tell you what's worrying me,' she said. 'It will be in all the papers this evening, I expect, anyway. You remember the murder of Perry Lamont at the Mammoth Picture Studios, don't you?'

Mr. Spearman started guiltily, but he managed to keep the shock he felt from appearing in his face as he answered quietly:

'Yes, but what has that got to do with you?'

'It's got nothing to do with me personally,' answered Mary, 'but the police have arrested my fiancé for the murder.'

Mr. Spearman's face expressed his amazement.

'Is that the man I've seen you about with?' he asked.

She nodded. 'Mr. Rennit — yes,' she replied. 'It's — it's dreadful, isn't it?'

'It sounds pretty bad,' said Mr. Spearman. 'Why should they have arrested him? What evidence have they got?'

'They found out that Dick quarrelled with Mr. Lamont,' she said, 'before the murder. And also — on the night that Mr. Lamont was killed — somebody saw him hanging round the Mammoth Studios.'

Tommy Spearman pursed up his lips.

'But that's not the worst of it,' she went on. 'Dick has — confessed that he killed Mr. Lamont.' Her eyes filled with tears and Mr. Spearman stared at her aghast.

This was the most amazing thing he had ever heard, for he was convinced in his own mind that Lefty Guinan was responsible for the death of Lamont. And now here was this girl telling him that her fiancé — what was his name? — Dick Rennit — had been arrested and had

111

actually confessed to the crime. It was seldom that he was so completely taken aback.

'But why should this fellow have killed Lamont?' he said. 'What was his motive?'

'I am — I am afraid that it was over me,' whispered Mary in a low voice, and she told him.

He listened sympathetically, but all the while his brain was working rapidly. There was something wrong here. In spite of Rennit's confession he felt that there was something wrong, and when she had finished he said:

'I'm terribly interested in this, Miss — ' He paused helplessly and looked at her.

'Henley,' she supplied.

'Miss Henley,' he went on. 'And if it's possible to do anything I'd like to do it. Suppose we have some lunch and see if anything can be done.'

She smiled through her tears.

'Thank you, I'd like to,' she said simply, 'but I thought you didn't eat lunch?'

'I'll break my rule for once,' said Mr. Spearman unselfishly. 'Let's go across to the Brown Derby.'

11

Rivington Recognises an Old Friend

Captain Willing's announcement came as something in the nature of a bombshell. Elmer Myers's jaw dropped and he remained staring at the police official with an expression of amazement that was really comic. Paul Rivington, although he showed it less, was every bit as astonished. Here were complications with a vengeance! There was a silence that was eventually broken by the managing director of Mammoth Pictures.

'Well, what you say beats everything!' he exclaimed, shaking his head.

'All the same, it's the truth,' answered Willing. 'We took Rennit this morning and he made no resistance.'

'And he actually confessed to the murder?' asked Paul, frowning.

'Sure he did, sir.' Captain Willing allowed a small note of triumph to creep into his voice. 'He confessed, and his confession was taken down in writing and he signed the statement. It was all voluntary; there was no third degree or anything like that.'

'What first put you on to Rennit?' asked Paul.

'When the murder was first made public,' replied Willing, 'a man came to the bureau and laid certain information. He said that he had seen two men quarrelling on Sunset Boulevard, and that he had recognised them. One was Perry Lamont and the other was this fellow Rennit. Rennit had knocked Lamont down and uttered a threat against his life. We made further inquiries, and discovered that there was a woman at the bottom of it — a girl called Mary Henley. She's a film extra, and apparently Lamont had been getting rather sweet on her. Offered to get her work under certain conditions. You know the usual guff. Well, Rennit was sweet on this girl, too, and there was bad feeling between the two men.'

'It seems to me rather a slender

foundation on which to have made an arrest,' said Rivington.

'I guess it would be if that had been all,' retorted Willing. 'But it wasn't all. Rennit was seen on the night of the murder hanging about outside the Mammoth Studios, and when we questioned him he refused to say what he was there for. Anyway, we've got the right man; he's admitted his guilt.'

Then he dropped a second bomb. A policeman on cycle patrol had been attracted to a disused studio by the sound of shots and had found Oscar Levenstein bleeding to death. Before he had died, however, he had named his assailants. They were Lefty Guinan and Spike Munro.

'The homicide squad are going up right away,' he said, 'and I'm joining them. The district attorney wants you and your brother to come along, Mr. Rivington.'

'Right you are,' agreed Paul. 'I'll come along with you. Are you coming, too, Myers?'

Elmer Myers shook his head.

'I can't,' he said. 'I've got to meet

Frank Leyland at the Brown Derby for lunch. Why not join us there after you've got through this business?'

'I will,' agreed Paul. 'Are you going now, Captain Willing?'

'Sure,' was the laconic reply.

'Come on, then,' said Paul, and both he and Bob followed the American detective to the high-powered police car that was waiting outside in the drive.

They started off, and halfway along the road to the disused studios where the tragedy had happened that morning the homicide squad car caught them up, carrying the district attorney, the district medical officer and men from the Central Office. They gave it priority along the narrow road that led up to the gate of the empty studios, and when they pulled up with the long radiator of the police car almost touching the rear lamp of the squad's car the occupants of the former had already descended and were standing in a little group before the wooden gate. Captain Willing introduced Rivington and his brother to the district attorney, and the grey-haired, stern-faced man shook hands heartily with both of them.

'Glad to meet you, Mr. Rivington,' he said. 'This is a terrible thing about poor Levenstein. We'll get the doctor's report and the man can take photographs.'

He called to a big man with badly fitting clothes, whom he introduced as Captain Benson.

'Benson's in charge of the case,' said the grey-haired man; 'you'd better get busy with your fellows, Benson.'

'OK,' said the other, and turning, he began ripping out orders.

The district attorney led the way towards the little gate and Paul and Bob followed.

As they passed into the courtyard Paul stood and watched while the routine methods adopted by the American police were put into operation. The district medical officer made his examination of the body and reported the result. Three bullets had torn their way through the chest and one of these had pierced the heart. Death had been almost instantaneous. One of the shots had passed completely through the body, and the bullet was found by one of

117

the men who had come with Captain Benson lying by the end wall of the yard. It was handed over for examination by the fire-arms expert, Captain Tandy.

When the first preliminary examination had been completed the photographers began their work. Several photographs were taken of the courtyard and body, and when this had been done the remains of Oscar Levenstein were carried out and put into the ambulance that had arrived in the interim. Paul Rivington was a great admirer of the efficiency and perfect organisation of the American detective force, and although he had seen it in action twice before, it never failed to interest him. There was very little difference in its methods from Scotland Yard, except that it had, to its advantage, a much freer hand, and was not bound by any restrictions and red tape.

When the ambulance had departed, carrying away the district medical officer, the district attorney brought Benson over to Paul.

As Myers had regretfully consented to it, Paul told about the theft of the film.

'Levenstein must have hired these guys to do the job for him,' said Benson as they drove back towards Hollywood in a police car. 'They're not local men. I know all the local crooks by sight, and I guess your description doesn't fit one of them.'

'Most probably they came from Chicago,' said the district attorney, and Benson nodded.

'I guess they did, sir,' he said. 'I'll get in touch with the Chicago Central Office and see if they can tell us anything about them.'

'We shall have the newsmen round here like flies over this murder,' said the district attorney with a frown. 'Levenstein's name makes a big story. Don't tell them anything about the film end to it, Benson.'

'I reckon you can trust me,' said the big man. 'I guess I'm not so fond of newsmen that I'm likely to spill anything more than I can help.'

'I suppose, Mr. Rivington,' said the district attorney, turning to Paul, who was seated on his other side, 'that you will still continue your search for this missing negative?'

'Yes,' answered Paul, 'that's really what I'm here for.'

'You can count on any assistance you may require from my department,' said the grey-haired man, 'and I'm sure Captain Benson will also give you all the help he can.'

'Sure I will,' said the officer heartily. 'Mr. Rivington has only got to say what he wants, and if I can give it to him it's his.'

Rivington tendered his thanks. The position of the district attorney in America is similar to that of the public prosecutor in England, with the exception that it is more of an executive job.

'The question at the moment,' said Paul, 'is what happened to the film. I'm pretty certain that Levenstein hadn't got it, and I'm equally certain that these two crooks haven't either. So who has got it?'

'Probably this guy Rennit could answer that,' put in Willing, who had been listening. 'He must have been in it with them.'

'I'd like to have a talk with him,' said

Paul, 'Could you arrange that?'

'Sure,' said Benson; 'he's in the cooler at Los Angeles, Come along this afternoon and I'll take you to see him.'

They fixed three o'clock, and then as they came in sight of the Brown Derby Paul asked them to stop the car; he and Bob got out, took their leave of the others, and when the car started once more went across and entered the doors of the famous restaurant. They saw Elmer Myers and Frank Leyland sitting at the table at the far end and joined them.

'Well,' greeted the managing director of Mammoth Pictures, 'what's happened?'

'Nothing very much,' answered Paul. 'Mostly routine, that's all. I want you to tell me something about this man Rennit. Is he the sort of fellow who would have been mixed up with these crooks who killed Levenstein?'

It was Frank Leyland who answered.

'I should say definitely no,' he declared. 'I'm not a friend of Rennit's, but I've met him several times at the studios, and I've met other people who know him quite well, and from all accounts he appears to be a very decent, hard-working chap. I can understand him killing Lamont if he had annoyed Mary Henley — that's the girl whom Rennit's taken keen on — but he wouldn't have joined up with any crooks to do it He'd have done it on his own and openly.'

Elmer Myers nodded.

'That's my view, too,' he confirmed.

'Well, I'm going to see him this afternoon,' said Paul, 'and I'd like to meet this girl too. Where can she be found?'

'Our casting director has got her address,' said Mr. Myers. 'I'll — '

'There she is now,' broke in Leyland. 'Just come in with that good-looking guy.'

Paul Rivington turned and looked in the direction the other had indicated, and the expression of his face changed.

'Who's the man with her?' he asked sharply, and Leyland shook his head.

'I don't know,' he replied. 'Do you, Elmer?'

'No, I guess he's a stranger to me,' said Mr. Myers.

'He's not a stranger to me,' said Paul shortly, and something in his tone made

Elmer Myers look at him quickly.

'Do you know him?' he asked.

'I know him rather well,' answered the detective. 'The last time I saw him was in the dock at the Old Bailey!'

12

Lefty Guinan Plans a Coup

Lefty Guinan and Spike faced each other over the table in their room at Mack's, and neither of their faces was pleasant to look upon.

'Say, what are we goin' to do now?' demanded Mr. Munro a little truculently, 'It's up to you to do somethin'.' He removed a chewed wad of gum from his mouth and substituted a fresh piece. 'This guy Spearman's got the film and he's got the money, an' we've got nothing. What are you going to do about it?'

'Shut up, and let me think!' snarled Lefty irritably.

'Sure I'll let you think all right,' said Spike, 'but I reckon you'd better not think too long. If we stop here it ain't goin' to be healthy.'

'That's what I'm thinkin' about, you fool,' broke in Lefty. 'I guess I know that as well as you do. But I'm not goin' back to Chicago until I've got even with Spearman.'

'Then what are you goin' to do?' asked Spike. 'We can't stop here or we'll be pinched.'

'We'll be pinched if we try to get away,' said Guinan. 'How far do you think we'd get on the train once our descriptions were circulated? Levenstein might have talked before he croaked. I didn't mean to kill Levenstein; I just lost my head.'

'If you waste time talkin' here you'll lose more than your head,' said Spike practically. 'See here, Lefty, we're up against it, and we've gotta think quick. The first thing we've gotta do is to get out of here.'

'That's all very well,' said Guinan, 'but where can we go?'

He began to walk up and down jerkily. There was something very like panic in his heart and he cursed himself again for his wild action in killing Oscar Levenstein and the lunacy that made him leave Spike alive to bear witness against him.

'We'll have to take to the road, Spike,'

he said, suddenly stopping, 'We've got the car, and if we can get out of the city into the country we'll at least have time to think.'

'Come on, then,' said Spike promptly. 'For the love of Mike let's get away from here.'

They decided that it was impossible to take their luggage, and Lefty hastily transferred what few papers he possessed from his big trunk to his breast pocket. With a self-possession they were far from feeling they walked down the stairs to the exit, but nobody took any notice of them. They reached the car, which Guinan had left outside, without being challenged. Lefty took his place at the wheel with a sigh of relief, and as he drove off with his companion beside him his forehead was wet with perspiration.

'One thing we can do,' he said as he swung the car into the main street. 'We can make some kind of a change in our appearance. Keep a look out for a drug store.'

Spike pointed out one a quarter of a mile further on — you can't travel far without finding a drug store in Hollywood — and Lefty stopped the car outside and entered the shop. He had no difficulty in purchasing what he wanted. The store was well stocked with materials for film make-up, and he rejoined the car feeling a little more cheerful. On the way out to the country they had to pass the Brown Derby, and as they went by the famous restaurant a man and a girl carne out.

'Look!' hissed Spike, clutching Lefty's arm. 'There's that guy Spearman with a dame!'

'I guess I'd like to get my own back on him,' he snapped viciously. 'Workin' with a girl, is he? That's a new one for Tommy. She's a good-looker too.'

He was hoping as the car went by that Mr. Spearman had not seen and recognised them. But about this he need not have worried. Tommy Spearman had for the moment forgotten that such people as Lefty Guinan and Spike Munro existed.

They came through the straggling outskirts of Culver City into open country, and in a rough and deserted patch of road Lefty pulled up the car and brought out the things he had bought at the drug store. With the aid of some anatto stain he gave himself a deep tan, and when he had shaved his eyebrows, brushed his hair in a different way and affixed a small moustache on his upper lip his appearance was so altered that even Spike had to look twice to be certain that it was still Lefty Guinan who sat beside him.

'You look swell,' he commented. 'You could walk past all the fly cops in Chicago and they'd never know you.'

'You'll be more difficult.' said Lefty, looking at Spike with his head on one side. 'But I reckon we can do something.'

He proceeded to do something. Spike had naturally thin eyebrows of a rather pale colour and these were augmented with false hair and darkened. At the same time their shape was altered — and nothing changes a person's looks so much as the shape of their eyebrows. A bottle of hair dye changed the mouse-coloured covering of Mr. Munro's head to a deep black. His pale complexion was made ruddy by the application of brick rouge. Lefty surveyed his work with satisfaction.

'I guess you'll do,' he grunted, and repacked his make-up materials. 'Now we've got to find somewhere to park ourselves.' He looked round at the countryside. 'I think we'll go on, and perhaps we can find some small apartment house or hotel where we can get a room.'

He started the engine and the car began to move forward again. The road got rougher, and presently led into another that wound its way along the foot of a chain of wooded hills. They had gone about half a mile along this when Guinan uttered an exclamation and stopped the car suddenly.

'What's bitin' you?' grumbled Spike.

Lefty took his right hand from the wheel and pointed towards the hills.

'Take a look at that,' he said.

Spike Munro twisted himself round in his seat and followed the direction of his companion's finger. Half-hidden among the trees he saw a house; at least it had obviously once been a house. Now it was more of a ruin than anything else. Only part of the roof still remained and the windows were broken. The paint was peeling from the doors and sashes, and about the whole place hung an atmosphere of neglect.

'Why stop to look at that?' grunted Mr. Munro disparagingly. 'I don't think much of it.'

'Don't you,' grinned Lefty. 'Well, I'm sorry, because I think we're going to see it at closer quarters.'

'Say, what's the idea?' said his companion.

'That's safer than all the apartment houses and hotels that were ever built,' said Lefty. 'I guess we can lie low there pretty secure.'

He swung himself out of the car.

'Come on, I'm going to have a look at the place.'

He went over to the gate, followed by the now-interested Spike. It was set well back from the road, a dilapidated affair that hung from one hinge and gave access to a twisting weed-choked path that wound its way up the hillside through an avenue of trees. The trees were so thick that from this point the house itself was completely invisible. When they eventually came in sight of it again they found that at closer quarters it was even in a worse state of repair than it had looked from the roadway. The sloping garden with its terraces was a riot of tangled weeds and flowers that had run to seed. The grass of the lawn was knee-deep, and the gravel of the path hidden in moss. Roses forlorn and neglected sprawled over broken trellis-work.

Lefty approached the porch and tried the door. It was locked, as he had expected, but the ground floor windows were so broken that the door as a barrier was more of a joke than anything else. He went round to the first window he came to and putting his hand through a large hole in one of the panes, jerked up the rusty catch. Opening the French windows, he stepped into a large low-roofed room that when the house had been inhabited had probably been the drawing room. The signs of neglect inside were even more evident than those without. The coloured wash on the walls was discoloured and thick with dirt; the ceiling had fallen in several places and lay in plaster heaps about the floor. The floor itself was no longer intact. Holes gaped everywhere.

'I guess you wouldn't call the place a palace,' grunted Spike Munro, looking about him and sniffing.

'What did you expect?' said Lefty. 'The Knickerbocker Building? I reckon we're darned lucky to have stumbled on this place. Let's see what the rest of it's like.'

They explored it thoroughly. It was not a very large house, but they found at least one room that was weatherproof, and this was the kitchen. It had a stone floor and was in better repair than any of the others.

'This is swell,' said Lefty. 'We can block up that window with sacks — ' He pointed to a heap of sacks that lay in one corner. ' — and nobody will be able to see a light.'

'What are we going to do about food?' demanded Mr. Munro, putting his last wad of gum into his mouth and thrusting it into his cheek.

'We'll get some canned stuff,' replied Lefty. 'Either you or I can go and get it. I guess we'd better not go together. There's less chance of our being recognised if we don't go together.'

'Sure. You go,' said Spike with alacrity.

'We'll toss up for it,' said Lefty Guinan, and put his hand in his pocket.

'Then we'll toss up with this,' said Mr. Munro emphatically and producing a dollar piece. 'I know that buck of yours, Lefty — both sides alike!'

He spun the coin and Guinan won.

'Away you go, Spike,' he said, grinning, 'and be as quick as you can.'

Mr. Munro departed, grumbling, and presently Lefty Guinan heard the whine of the car as it faded in the distance. While the other was gone Lefty occupied his time by covering the window with sacking and making everything as comfortable as he could. When he had finished he sat down on a box which he had found in the cellar and lit a cigarette. His thoughts turned to Tommy Spearman and his heart was savage at the way he had been twisted. He'd have given a lot to be even with that gentleman — he didn't call him a gentleman in his mind — and get his money back. It wasn't that he was broke, but he was precious near it, near enough in fact to be unpleasant, and if he was ever going to get out of the mess he'd got himself into and see Chicago once more he would need money, and lots of it.

Sitting in the bare empty kitchen, frowning and smoking, an idea came to him. It came flashing like a ray of light on a dark night, and Lefty Guinan drew a deep breath. If only it could be done. Not only would it get his money back — at least, knowing something of Mr. Spearman's character he was pretty sure it would — but he could probably get the film as well. Yes, it was certainly a swell idea, and the more he thought of it the more he liked it. Not very difficult either. Now they'd found this house it would be easy. In his imagination he saw the idea put into practice, and his mouth curled into a cruel smile. He'd make Tommy Spearman squirm. He should suffer for what he'd done.

Spike Munro, coming back laden with

parcels, found him almost jubilant.

'What's got you?' he asked, eyeing his companion suspiciously.

'I've got a swell plan — ' began Lefty.

'Well, keep it to yourself,' said Mr. Munro. 'It's your swell plans that have landed us in this mess.'

Lefty Guinan's face darkened.

'Cut that stuff!' he snarled. 'I'm not standin' any of that from you, Spike, so get that in your head! Can I help the luck goin' against me? This idea of mine's fine and dandy, and it'll put us on velvet again.'

'If it'll do that, spill it,' said Spike.

Rapidly Lefty Guinan explained his great scheme, and when he had finished Spike Muro nodded.

'I'll hand it to you, Lefty,' he said. 'It's a swell idea!'

13

The Con Man

'A crook, is he?' said Elmer Myers, raising his eyebrows. 'Are you sure you haven't made a mistake?'

Paul shook his head and shifted his position so that he was next to Elmer Myers and not in a direct line of sight with the man who had come in.

'No, I've made no mistake,' he said. 'That fellow's name is Tommy Spearman, and when I saw him he was on trial for fraud.'

Frank Leyland frowned.

'What the deuce is Mary Henley doing with a fellow like that?' he muttered. 'She's not that sort.'

'Probably she doesn't know his real character,' said Paul. 'I hope he hasn't spotted me.'

He need not have worried. Mr. Spearman sat down at a table near the door with his back to the detective and became at once engrossed in his pretty companion.

Paul Rivington watched them and wondered. What had brought Tommy Spearman to Hollywood, and what was he doing with this girl who was the fiancée of the man held for the murder of Perry Lamont? Was he in this business of the stolen film too? Paul decided that Mr. Spearman would be worth keeping an eye on. There was a possibility that they were all in it — Rennit, the girl, and Spearman. Perhaps the two crooks who had shot Levenstein had been engaged by Spearman to steal the film, and had tried to double-cross him. It was all a bit complicated and would require thinking out, but it certainly looked as if Spearman was connected with the business in some way, and therefore a good standpoint. The girl and he were talking in low tones, and Paul would have given a lot to know what it was they were talking about. Presently when they had finished their lunch they rose to go, and as they reached the door Paul leaned forward and touched his brother's arm.

'Slip along after them, old chap,' he whispered, 'and find out if you can where Spearman is staying and what name he's using. It's certainly not his own.'

Bob nodded and, rising, sauntered over to the door and made his exit in the wake of Mr. Spearman and the girl. He had not very far to go, for outside the Beverley Wilshire Mr. Spearman and the girl halted. They chatted for a second or two and then parted, she to go down the street and he to turn into the hotel. Bob waited for five or six minutes, then he crossed the road, ascended the steps of the Beverley Wilshire, and approached the reception clerk's desk.

'Have you a gentleman named Mr. Lickerbolt staying here?' he asked.

'What name?' asked the clerk. 'Lickerbolt,' repeated Bob — it was the most unusual name he could think of on the spur of the moment.

The reception clerk shook his head.

'Nope,' he replied. 'I guess nobody of that name is stayin' here.'

'But I'm sure he said he was staying here,' persisted Bob, frowning. 'Perhaps you'd recognise him if I described him to you.'

He gave a description that might have fitted Mr. Spearman, without the small physical alterations that he purposely put in.

'That sounds like Captain Chase,' said the clerk at once. 'He's an Englishman . . .'

'Then he wouldn't be my friend,' said Bob. 'My friend's an American. Besides, his name's Lickerbolt, and there's no reason for him to change it.'

'I guess if I had a name like that,' replied the clerk, 'I'd darn soon change it!'

Bob grinned, thanked him, apologised for troubling him and went back to the Brown Derby.

'Well, that's quick work, anyway,' said Paul, when his brother told him what had happened. 'So Captain Chase is the name he's going under, is it? That sounds very Spearmanish.' He glanced at his watch. 'I must be getting along to Los Angeles to see Rennit. Listen, Bob; you stop around here and keep an eye on Captain Chase.

I'm interested in that gentleman's movements.'

'You reckon he's mixed up in this business,' asked Elmer Myers.

'I think it's more than likely,' answered Paul. 'I don't know how, but that's what I'm hoping to find out.'

'Leyland and I are going to the studios,' said Myers, 'and after that I'm going home. I'll see you there.'

Paul agreed, and they left the restaurant. Outside the detective took leave of the others and drove down to the Central Detective Bureau at Los Angeles. He arrived a little before the time of his appointment, but he found Captain Benson waiting for him

'I guess I've got news for you, Mr. Rivington,' he said, leading the way into his office. 'We've succeeded in getting pictures of those two crooks of yours.'

'They're not my special property, you know,' said Paul, smiling.

Benson's large face creased into a grin.

'Sure they're not,' he answered. 'I guess they knew all about them in Chicago, and nothing to their credit. He displayed one of the photographs that had arrived by telegraph. 'The smaller man is Spike Munro and the big 'un is Lefty Guinan. They've been mixed up in all sorts of shady business, and were well in with Lew Healey and the rum-runners for some time.'

'Well, that's good work,' said Paul, 'and the next thing to do is to pull them in.'

'And I guess it won't be long before we do that,' declared Benson confidently. 'I've got men stationed at the railroad stations so they can't very well leave the city. And I've got a whole squad of men combing the apartment houses and the hotels. I don't reckon it'll be long before they're run to earth.' He pushed a box of black cigars across to Paul, but the other declined the invitation.

'I'd rather have a cigarette, if you don't mind,' he said, producing his case and taking one out. 'Tell me, have you ever heard of a man called Tommy Spearman?'

Benson helped himself to a cigar, bit off the end, frowned and shook his head.

'No,' he replied. 'Who is he?'

'He's an English crook,' said the

detective. 'One of the cleverest confidence men I know, and he's in Hollywood staying at the Beverley Wilshire under the name of Captain Chase.'

'Oh, is that the guy?' said Benson. 'Of course, we know of his arrival. We check up all strangers that come to the city, but we couldn't find anything wrong with him.'

'You wouldn't,' declared Paul. 'Tommy Spearman would take care of that. But the fact that he's here rather interests me.'

He told the other under what conditions he had seen Mr. Spearman, and Benson scratched the lowest of his many chins.

'I guess it sounds a bit complicated,' he remarked. 'Here are these two fellers, Munro and Guinan, who we know killed Levenstein and did the bust at Mammoth Studios. Here's Rennit, who swears he killed Lamont, and now here's this guy you're talkin' about, all friendly with Rennit's girl. How many more of them are in this business, and who's got the film?'

'That,' said Paul, 'is a question that

interests me, since it's my job to find it. I don't know how they all come into it, but I don't mind betting that Spearman's got the film.'

'What makes you think that?' asked Benson.

'Well, who else can have it?' said Paul. 'It was never given to Levenstein, and he never stole it from Guinan. I'm certain of that, and equally certain that Guinan hasn't got it. There's a chance that Rennit might have it, but I don't think so. And, anyhow, knowing Spearman as I do, he's the most likely. If he was in with them on this business, it's just the sort of thing he would do, and try and make a bit on his own.'

'Well, I reckon it won't be difficult to find out,' said Captain Benson, blowing a cloud of smoke across his desk. 'You say he's staying at the Beverley Wilshire? I'll have a man sent to search his apartments.'

'That's what I was going to suggest,' said the detective, 'and I'd like to go with him if I may.'

'Sure you may,' agreed the other. 'This

film is part of the job. Would you like me to arrange for the man to go back with you after you've seen Rennit?'

'Yes, if you can manage it,' said Rivington.

'Sure I can,' declared Benson. 'Now come along, and I'll shoot you into this fellow Rennit.'

He rose and Paul followed him out of the office through the building to the part where the cells were situated. Dick Rennit, pale, haggard and unshaven, looked up with weary eyes as they entered. He was sitting dejectedly on the pallet-bed, his hands clasped loosely between his knees.

'This gentleman wants to have a talk with you, Rennit,' said Benson, and Dick's face set.

'Why can't you leave me alone?' he demanded hoarsely. 'I've told you all you want to know, haven't I? I've told you I killed Lamont. What more do you want?'

'Quite a lot,' said Paul. 'I want to ask you one or two questions — '

'I won't answer any questions,' said Rennit sullenly. 'Questions, questions, questions! Great Heaven, nothing but questions! Can't you leave me alone? I've told you all I'm going to tell you. I've made a statement and signed it. All you want to know is who killed Lamont, and I've told you — I did. Now leave me alone!'

His nerves were on edge, and Rivington privately came to the conclusion that he was not far off hysteria. He tried to adopt a soothing tone, but it had no effect. For nearly an hour he questioned, suggested and tried by every device he could think of to get Rennit to talk, but without success. All he would do was to keep on reiterating that he had killed Lamont. Paul gave it up at last and accompanied Benson back to the latter's office.

'Well, what do you make of him?' asked the captain.

'He's so insistent he killed Lamont,' replied Paul thoughtfully, 'that one's almost inclined to think he did nothing of the kind.'

Captain Benson looked at him sharply.

'Queer you should say that,' he remarked, 'because I've thought the same thing. I guess his great trouble seems to be that we might not believe him.'

'In which case you would, of course, start looking for somebody else,' said Paul. 'That's what troubling Rennit; he's shielding somebody.'

'Who could he be shielding?' asked Benson, wrinkling his forehead.

'There's only one person so far as I can see,' replied Rivington, 'and that's the girl — Mary Henley!'

14

Mr. Spearman Scores

Mr. Thomas Spearman, alias Captain Chase, was feeling cheerful when he left Mary Henley and ascended to his comfortable suite of rooms at the Beverley Wilshire. He had plenty of money and the means for acquiring more, and he had made the acquaintance of a girl who for the first time in his chequered career had the power to make his pulse beat a little quicker. He tried, as he sat down by the open window of his sitting room, to think of a word that would describe her, and rejected superlative after superlative. In his younger days — before he had been cashiered from a crack regiment for copying the signature of a fellow-officer on one of the latter's cheques — Mr. Spearman had had dreams. He had in his more serious moments visualised just the kind of girl he would have liked to marry and settle down with. In the years that followed these dreams had grown more shadowy and remote, until they had almost faded altogether. And now — here was the epitome of his visions, a living, breathing reality. Mr. Spearman sighed and lit a cigarette.

Of course, it was too late now. Apart from the fact that Mary Henley was obviously deeply wrapped up in Dick Rennit, she could never be anything to him. To give him his due, he would never have dreamed of asking her, even if she had been free. His was not the kind of life that a woman could share, and he had no illusions that marriage would reform him. He was a crook by nature and inclination, and a crook he would be until the hour of his death. All the same, it was pleasant to talk to her, even though it was and could never be anything else but a passing interlude. He had promised to do all he could to help her, and he was quite genuine about this.

Of course, if Rennit had killed Lamont, there was nothing he could do. The question was, had he? There seemed no reason why the young fool should have confessed unless he had.

He frowned and thought hard, but by tea-time he had come to no satisfactory conclusion. The English habit of tea still clung to him, and he went down to the lounge to order some. As he passed the reception clerk the man smiled and, calling to him, handed him a bundle of English newspapers. Mr. Spearman, who was interested in the doings of his country, had ordered them.

'You've got a double, Captain Chase,' said the clerk. 'I guess you didn't know that.'

'Have I?' said Mr. Spearman not very interested. 'Who is the unfortunate person?'

'A guy called Lickerbolt,' said the man with a grin, and related his conversation with Bob.

Mr. Spearman's interest increased suddenly. This looked a little disconcerting. There might, of course, be nothing in it, but on the other hand there might. Adopting a bored air, he cautiously questioned the reception clerk and succeeded in extracting from him a description of Bob, It was not a very good description, and conveyed nothing at all to Mr. Spearman, but it left him rather alert.

'Why, there's the guy now, sir,' said the clerk just as he was turning away to the lounge. 'On the other side of the street. Still looking for his friend, I expect.'

Mr. Spearman glanced through the glass doors of the entrance, and it was only by an effort that he succeeded in retaining his composure.

'Oh, is that the chap!' he said smoothly, and wondered if the clerk could hear the pounding of his heart. 'Well, I hope he finds this fellow — what's-his-name — Lickerbolt.'

He smiled, nodded and turned away. He did not go to the lounge as he had originally intended. Instead he went back to his sitting room. If Bob Rivington was in Hollywood it meant that his brother was there also and they were obviously interested in him. Mr. Spearman felt a little perturbed. What was the reason for this sudden interest, and why were they there at all? He walked up and down the comfortable room uneasily. They couldn't have got anything on him. Lefty Guinan dared not have given him away, either about the money or the film. So what was the meaning of this attention on Bob Rivington's part? The story of Mr. Lickerbolt was all nonsense, of course. It had been a ruse to find out if he were staying at the Beverley Wilshire.

And now they had found out they were watching the place. Mr. Spearman's face was very serious. Although he couldn't understand what it was, there was something up, and he decided that he ought to take precautions. During the next fifteen minutes his brain worked very rapidly indeed, and presently he came to a conclusion.

He proceeded to put this into execution at once, and felt easier when he had done so. Once more he began to think about his tea, and rang the bell. To the waiter who answered the ring he gave his order, and presently was sipping his tea and munching the anchovy toast that accompanied it. Although he had still one or two qualms, he was feeling considerably more comfortable, and when he had swallowed his second cup and lit a cigarette he had come to the conclusion that it was very doubtful whether Rivington could do anything to cause him inconvenience. He had almost reached the end of his cigarette when there came a tap at the door, and in answer to his 'Come in' a bellboy entered.

'Two gentlemen want to see you, sir,' he said, and Mr. Spearman, who had expected the waiter to take away the tea-tray, raised his eyebrows in surprise.

'Two gentlemen?' he repeated. 'To see me? Who are they?'

'They didn't give any names,' answered the bellboy, 'but I can tell you who one of them is — Captain Willing, from the police.'

Mr. Spearman kept his face expressionless, although the shock had been no light one.

'What on earth can he want to see me for?' he muttered in the puzzled tones of an honest man who cannot imagine why anyone connected with the police should desire to make his acquaintance. 'Anyway, I suppose you'd better show them up.'

The bellboy departed, and Mr. Spearman braced himself for the coming interview.

He thanked his lucky stars that his caution had prompted him to do what he had done, if he had been taken unawares — he gave a little shiver. He had tasted prison-life, and had no wish to repeat the experience. There came another tap at me door, and this time the bellboy ushered in two men. The first was a complete stranger to Mr. Spearman, but the second — there was no mistaking the other man, it was Paul Rivington.

'Good afternoon, Mr. Spearman,' said Paul pleasantly. 'Sorry to disturb you, but we would like to have a word with you.'

Tommy Spearman, without much hope that it would do any good, decided to try and bluff it out.

'I'm afraid you're making a mistake, aren't you?' he said, frowning a little. 'My name is Chase — Garvin Chase — '

'Is it, now?' said Paul gently. 'I'm not a bit surprised to hear that, Tommy. If I'd called on you a month ago it would probably have been something else. Where do you get all these names from — the telephone directory?'

Mr. Spearman's frown deepened.

'I assure you that you're making a mistake,' he said with quiet dignity. 'I can prove to you — '

'You can prove anything to me except that you're not Tommy Spearman,' broke in the detective smoothly. 'It's no good bluffing, I know you far too well. You've got a bayonet wound under your right shoulder-blade, and two shrapnel scars on your thigh.'

Mr. Spearman accepted his defeat gracefully and shrugged his shoulders.

'You win, Rivington,' he said with a wry smile, 'but I don't know what you've come up for. You've got nothing on me.'

'That remains to be seen,' answered Paul. 'We've reason to believe that you were connected with the robbery at the Mammoth Pictures Studios and the murder of Perry Lamont.'

'What robbery?' demanded Mr. Spearman quickly. 'I've heard of the murder, of course — everybody within a radius of ten miles has talked about nothing else — but I didn't know there was a robbery.'

'No, of course you wouldn't,' said Paul with a smile. 'Very clever, Tommy. Well, there was a robbery.'

'I'm afraid you've come after the wrong fox, Rivington,' said Mr. Spearman. 'I had nothing to do with that business — either robbery or murder. Anyhow, I thought you'd got the fellow who killed Lamont all safely locked up.'

'You shouldn't think so much, Tommy,' said Paul. 'We're not satisfied that Rennit did kill Lamont.'

'Well, I know nothing about it,' declared Mr. Spearman. 'As a matter of fact, Rivington, I've given up all that stuff. I'm going straight now — '

'I thought at least you'd be original, Tommy,' interrupted Paul reproachfully. 'That's what every little sneak-thief always says. It's the first thing they learn at school.'

'I know you don't believe me,' retorted Mr. Spearman virtuously, 'but there you are. If you can prove anything against me, you're welcome. I say that with a clear conscience.'

'Well, we'll see,' said Paul. 'Have you any objection to us making a search of this suite?'

'Not if you've got a warrant — ' began

Mr. Spearman, and was interrupted by Captain Willing.

'I guess we've got that all right,' he said grimly.

'Then carry on,' said Mr. Spearman with a graceful wave of his hand. 'I hope you don't mind if I smoke.'

Without waiting for permission he perched himself on the arm of an easy-chair. Paul and Willing began a systematic search. They turned out the wardrobe and went through all Mr. Spearman's luggage. They peered into every nook and cranny of the two rooms and bathroom which comprised the suite, and they found — nothing.

'Found anything?' asked Tommy Spearman blandly when they came back rather hot and dishevelled to the sitting room.

'Nothing,' said Paul Rivington sternly.

'I told you you wouldn't, you know,' said Mr. Spearman. 'If you'd listened to me you'd have saved yourself a lot of trouble — '

'You haven't deposited anything with the management, have you?' broke in the detective, frowning.

'No,' drawled Mr. Spearman, shaking his head.

'I'll have to ask him,' said Paul.

'Ask him by all means, my dear fellow,' said the other. 'I'll ring the bell.'

He strolled lazily across the room and did so, and the manager, when he had been sent for, bore out this statement. Captain Chase had deposited nothing with the hotel.

'Satisfied?' enquired Mr. Spearman when they were once more alone.

'No,' snapped Paul irritably. He had expected better results than this, and he was annoyed.

'Might I enquire,' said Mr. Spearman interestedly, 'what exactly did you expect to find?'

'I expected to find the negative of a film,' was the answer. 'What have you done with it?'

Tommy Spearman's expression was one of innocent surprise as he looked at his questioner.

'The negative of a film?' he repeated. 'My dear fellow, what are you talking about? I know nothing about films.'

'Apparently,' answered Paul dryly. 'Well, I suppose we'll have to give you a clean bill for the time being, but I shouldn't advise you to try and leave the city.'

'I've no intention of leaving it,' declared Mr. Spearman. 'It's the most delightful place, and the air agrees with my constitution.'

He waited for an hour after they had gone, and then strolling out into the corridor he made his way to the service lift. It was only in use during morning and evening as he very well knew, and now it was out of sight. Pressing the button that set it in motion, he waited for it to appear, and presently it came slowly into view and stopped. Mr. Spearman raised himself on tiptoe, and putting his hand into the space at the top of the gate, felt about on the roof of the lift. He withdrew, one at a time, seven round flat tin boxes, and tucking them under his arm, returned to his suite humming a tune.

15

Lefty Guinan Strikes

Mary Henley had a tiny room at the top of a tall apartment house in Culver City. It was really a bijou flat, for it contained a microscopic kitchenette and bathroom as well. These were more like large cupboards than separate rooms. She had great difficulty in finding the small rental that was demanded for this habitation, but had succeeded in doing so somehow. But how long she would be able to continue was a matter for a great deal of speculation.

Irene Claremont had a larger flat in the same building, and the two girls were in the habit of pooling their resources for catering, which made the food problem a little cheaper. They took it in turns to have meals with each other. One day Mary would go down to Irene's flat and the next Irene would come up to hers. On the night following her meeting with Mr. Spearman Mary should have gone down to Irene, but when she got home she found a note waiting for her, saying that her friend had a bad headache and had gone to bed.

Mary was a little thankful. She felt that she would rather be alone. She was very worried, and she had a lot to think about, and although she quite liked Irene she was not terribly attached to her. Her slightly affected manner got on her nerves at times, and she felt that this would have been one of the times.

She made herself some tea and boiled some eggs — all that she could find in the small larder — and ate her meal a little wearily. She was desperately tired — not physically but mentally — but she knew that if she went to bed she would only lie awake for hours.

Dick's attitude bewildered and hurt her. Ever since the murder of Lamont he had changed and done his best to avoid her, and now that he had been arrested he refused point-blank to see her. She couldn't believe that he was really guilty of the crime, although he had admitted it. There must be some mistake somewhere, and yet perhaps he had killed Lamont after all. If he had, she felt to a great extent responsible, for it must have been on her account.

She finished her supper, washed up the dishes, and sat herself down in the single armchair her little apartment boasted. It was only nine o'clock, as she saw with dismay, when she glanced at her watch. Before she could go to bed with any hope of sleep she would have to fill in two hours at least. She picked up a book she had been reading, and was halfway through, and tried to forget her worries and concentrate on the story. But although she read diligently every word of two pages she found that they possessed no meaning for her, and at last she laid the book down and let her thoughts come crowding back as they would.

Perhaps Captain Chase could do something. He had promised that he would help her if he could. He had been terribly kind. He had arranged to take her to lunch tomorrow. Perhaps he would be able to suggest something then. If only Dick would see her. Why did he want to behave like this? Did he blame her for the position he was in? This was an aspect that had not occurred to her before, and she thought it out. Perhaps that was what it was. He had killed Lament because of her, and now he blamed her for it.

If that was the case, it was rather unfair. She kept on going over the same ground again and again until her head ached, and presently, although it was barely half-past ten, she rose to go to bed. She felt tired enough, Heaven knew. Perhaps sleep would come if she tried to woo it.

She was just starting to undress when the telephone rang. She looked at the instrument and frowned. Who could be calling up at that hour? And then an idea occurred to her. Perhaps it was Captain Chase. She'd given him the number. She went quickly across to the instrument and lifted the receiver.

'Hello!' she called, and a strange voice answered her over the wire.

'Hello!' it said gruffly. 'I'm speaking for Mr. Spearman.'

'Mr, Spearman? I'm afraid you've got the wrong number,' she said.

There was a moment's pause, and then the voice went on:

'That's Avenue 900, isn't it?'

'Yes, but I don't know anybody called Mr. Spearman,' said Mary.

This time there was a longer pause.

'I mean the gentleman you were with this morning,' said the voice at last.

'Oh, Captain Chase — yes?' she waited expectantly.

'That's the guy, miss,' said the man at the other end of the wire. 'I guess I made a mistake. I had two calls to make and I mixed up the names. Captain Chase says, could you meet him on Sunset Boulevard in half an hour?'

She thought quickly.

'What part of Sunset Boulevard?' she asked.

'Just walk slowly along towards Los Angeles,' said the stranger, 'and Captain Chase will pick you up. He says it's rather urgent.'

'All right — tell him I'll be there,' she promised, and heard the click of the receiver as the man at the other end rang off.

Hurriedly she left the telephone and put on the few garments she had taken off when the call disturbed her. She would have to hurry, for it would take nearly half an hour to reach Sunset Boulevard. She wondered, while she made her preparations for departure, why he had chosen such an extraordinary meeting place. Why hadn't he fixed a definite place like the Brown Derby or his own hotel?

She came to the conclusion that for some reason or other he did not want their meeting to be public. This filled her with curiosity to know why, and occupied her mind with speculation as she walked towards the broad thoroughfare which is the pride of California. There were one or two cars speeding by on the well-kept road, but few people about, for at that hour most of the film colony were in bed and sleeping in preparation for the morrow's work.

Mary walked slowly, keeping a sharp lookout for the tall, slim figure of Captain Chase. She had gone nearly a quarter of a mile when she saw a car coming slowly towards her. It was travelling close to the sidewalk, and as she came level with it, it stopped. It was a small car with the hood up, and as it came to a halt a man thrust his head out from the interior.

'You lookin' for Captain Chase?' he asked in a loud whisper.

'Yes,' she began doubtfully. 'Why — '

'You get in beside me, Miss,' said the man in the car, 'an' I'll take you to him.'

There was a click as he opened the door invitingly. She hesitated, some instinct — that animal instinct which is possessed by everyone, but which civilisation has nearly succeeded in smothering — warned her of danger.

'Be quick!' said the driver of the car impatiently. 'Captain Chase is waiting and it's very urgent.'

Mary thrust down her fears and approaching the car got in.

'Shut the door, will you?' said the man behind the wheel as she took her seat beside him. She complied, and then turned to ask a question.

'Where — ' she began and then a hand

came up and gripped her throat and another was pressed over her nose and mouth. She struggled violently — tearing with her nails at the hands and wrists of her assailant. But he was wearing thick gloves and she made no impression.

The imprisoned breath in her lungs was making her head swim and she felt as though her forehead was bursting, and then mercifully blackness swamped her senses and she slumped forward in the seat unconscious.

★   ★   ★

A cold wind blowing on her face was the first sensation she experienced when she came slowly back to consciousness. The second was the dim murmur of voices.

She opened her eyes and stared up into the open sky. She could see a myriad stars flecking the deep blue vault above, and found she was lying in some kind of long grass. She turned her head and tried to see more of the place where she was, but she could see nothing but a vague outline of bushes and the tall blades of grass that clustered thickly round her. The murmur of voices came again, but she could not hear what was being said. She tried to move, but found that this was impossible, because her hands and feet had been securely tied.

She felt rather frightened. She remembered getting into the car and the hand that had gripped her throat and choked her into insensibility — her throat was still sore from that merciless grasp — but why had it all happened? What was the object?

She was given very little time to wonder, for she heard the swish of feet coming through the grass, and presently saw the figures of two men loom above her.

'You take her head, and I'll take her feet, Spike,' grunted the voice she had heard on the telephone.

They stooped and lifted her, and now that she was clear of the surrounding grass that had hedged her in, she could see the dim bulk of a house of some kind. Towards this her two captors carried her, stumbling over the rough ground. She was able to catch a glimpse of a broken window and a dilapidated veranda, and then they passed through a door and their footsteps rang on bare boards. The house, or whatever it was, was empty. She could tell that by the musty smell that came to her nostrils. They negotiated a passage, passed through another door, and laid her down roughly on a stone floor in a room that was lit by two candles stuck in their own grease on the mantelpiece.

She had as yet given no sign that her senses had come back to her, and now she still kept her eyes almost closed, taking stock of her surroundings through narrow slits veiled by her lashes.

'Well, that's swell,' said the man who had spoken before. 'I reckon it was a very neat bit of work.'

'What's the next move?' asked the other man.

'I guess the next move is to ring up Spearman,' was the reply. 'We'll fix this dame up nice and comfy, and then I'll go along and do that.'

He came over and stood looking down at her, and it was all she could do to suppress the shudder of fear that went through her as she saw his face — dark and cruel.

'She's a good-looker; I've said it before and I'll say it again,' said Lefty Guinan. 'A swell baby! Spearman sure knows how to pick 'em.'

He turned away, and Mary, completely puzzled, wondered what he was talking about. Who was Spearman? She knew nobody of that name, and yet these men talked as if they were intimate. Had they made a mistake, and kidnapped her believing she was someone else? It didn't seem likely, since they had got her right telephone number. The next words of the man who had brought her to this unpleasant place were even more puzzling.

'This will make him part,' he said, with a note of satisfaction in his voice. 'I guess before morning we'll have the money and the film.'

'I hope you're right,' grunted his companion, and produced from his pocket a packet of chewing-gum.

'Sure I'm right,' said the other confidently. 'When we've got what we want out of him — ' His voice changed to a menacing snarl. ' — then we'll make him pay for all the trouble we've been put to.'

Mary Henley heard the cold ferocity in his tone and shuddered.

16

Mr. Spearman Walks Into a Trap

'So, I shall be very glad, Captain — er — Chase, if you will make it convenient to leave tomorrow,' said the manager of the Beverley Wilshire suavely. 'It is my duty to study my clients and — '

'And you think that my presence will corrupt their morals,' said Spearman, lolling back in his chair perfectly at ease. 'Well, probably it would do some of them good if I did. For a more dull and stodgy lot I've never come across!'

The urbane manager's face expressed his horror at this sacrilege.

'People who stay here are very select,' he said stiffly.

'I'd like to know who selects them,' replied Tommy Spearman. 'By the look of 'em I should think they'd select themselves! However, don't worry. Although there's nothing whatever against me, I will remove my undesirable presence in the morning.'

The manager looked relieved.

'I guess we're very sorry, Captain Chase,' he said, 'but I'm sure you understand. A visit from the police is liable to be misconstrued, even if there is no foundation for their suspicion — '

An imp of mischief prompted Mr. Spearman to try and shock this solid and complacent man.

'Their suspicions had a very solid foundation,' he said calmly. 'I don't mind telling you — now I've got to change my plans — that I had every intention of burgling the hotel tonight.'

'You — were going — to rob the hotel?' The manager almost swooned with horror at the suggestion. 'You — you can't be serious!'

'Why not?' said Mr. Spearman. 'If you'll look at those bills which have been brought me since I have been here and which I have paid you'll see that the hotel has been robbing me for nearly a month. Why shouldn't I do a little stealing on my own account?'

The manager cleared his throat.

'I prefer to think that you're joking, Captain Chase,' he said with great dignity, 'and I should be glad to know what time you will be leaving in the morning.'

'Immediately after breakfast,' said Mr. Spearman. 'Tell them to call me at eight.'

'The floor waiter will attend to that.' The manager concealed his outraged dignity at being given an order by a stiff little bow. 'Good evening, Captain Chase.'

'Good evening,' answered Mr. Spearman, 'and don't forget to put a notice up, telling all the residents to double-lock their doors tonight.'

The manager withdrew without making any reply, and Mr. Spearman settled himself more comfortably in his chair. He had expected the visit that had just been made, and had therefore been prepared for it, and although he had carried it off lightly, it was going to be deuced awkward.

Hidden away in the bottom of one of his big trunks was the film, and if he moved and Rivington decided to search his luggage again it couldn't fail to be found. At all costs he must guard against that, and think out some scheme by which he could successfully get rid of the thing.

His plan for negotiating with Mammoth Pictures for its return would in any case have to be postponed. He could not put that into practice until he was in a safer position himself. In the meanwhile the film would have to be deposited in a safe place.

He got up, helped himself to a cigarette, and sat down again. Now, what could he do with it?

If he took it outside the hotel it was practically certain that he would be stopped. He knew Rivington sufficiently well to be sure that the detective would not be satisfied by the fact that he had found nothing in his suite. He was thorough; given the slightest suspicion, he would hang on like a bulldog until he had either confirmed it or found that he was wrong. So there was very little doubt that the Beverley Wilshire was under observation. Mr. Spearman wrinkled his brows. One thing, however, was certain — he must get rid of that film before he left in the morning.

He thought of everything, but without success, and then just as he was beginning to think it was hopeless he got an idea. Of course; it was simple. Why hadn't he thought of it before?

He got up, went into the bedroom, and locking the door opened the trunk in which he had put the film and brought it out. Putting it on the table, he found brown paper and string and made the boxes up into a neat parcel. Carefully he addressed it: 'John Clayton, Esq., Central Post Office, Los Angeles. To be called for.' He surveyed his handiwork with satisfaction, and unlocking the door, went back to the sitting room and rang the bell. After a short delay the floor waiter answered the summons.

'I want you to have this parcel sent off for me,' said Mr. Spearman. 'It's rather important, so I wish you'd see to it yourself.'

He pulled a ten-dollar bill from his pocket and gave it to the man.

'This will compensate you for any trouble.'

The man was effusive in his thanks. He

would be going off duty in a quarter of an hour and would see that the parcel was posted. He bowed himself out, and as the door closed Tommy Spearman sighed with relief.

Well, that was that! The film would now rest safely in the care of the postal officials of Los Angeles, waiting for him to collect it, and when it was safe to do so, all he had to do was to go and pick it up. He congratulated himself on his good idea. With great cheerfulness he had a bath, dressed himself, and a little after eight strolled across to the Brown Derby for dinner. The place was crowded as usual, and Mr. Spearman looked about him with peace and contentment in his soul, and no shadow or premonition of the future came to him; no warning voice spoke of the fate that was lurking in wait for him, no writing on the wall forecast that this was to be the last dinner he was ever destined to eat.

He enjoyed that meal, chose it with care, and lingered over each course, watching and listening to the happy chattering throng that surrounded him.

Halfway through he wished that he had rung up Mary Henley and asked her to join him. He sat over his coffee and cigar for a long time, until, in fact, the place was beginning to empty, and then reluctantly — for his suite at the hotel would seem very cheerless and lonely after this bright oasis — he rose, paid his bill, and slowly strolled back to the Beverley Wilshire.

He looked about sharply for any possible watchers, but he saw none. The time was half-past ten when he reached his suite. Slipping off his dinner jacket, he pulled on a dressing gown, mixed himself a whisky and soda, and with the glass in his hand went over to the window and stood looking out on to the Wilshire Boulevard. Cars were passing to and fro in the street below and the neon signs flashing. His mind went back to the morning of his arrival, when he had stood as he stood now and made plans. Well, so far his stay in Hollywood had been a profitable one. He drained his glass and went back to the table for another. He'd never felt so wakeful in his life, and going back to the window, he watched for half an hour, until the traffic had gradually ceased. And then remembering that he had scarcely looked at the bundle of English newspapers that had arrived for him that day, he collected them and settled down to peruse the news they contained.

It was half-past twelve when he tossed the last one aside, and stretched himself with a yawn. It was a long time since he had seen the Old Country, walked down Piccadilly and Bond Street, and watched the riders in the Row. It would not be a bad idea to go back. America was all right; New York was gay, Chicago was worth seeing, and Hollywood was beautiful, but London took a lot of beating.

The telephone bell purred softly, and he started up and looked at the instrument. Who the deuce could be ringing him so late? He went over and lifted the receiver; the voice of the switchboard girl came to his ears.

'Captain Chase?' she twanged, and when he replied in the affirmative, 'there's a call for you. Just a moment, please.'

There was the click of a plugged-in switch, and then a man's voice:

'Hello! Captain Chase?'

'Yes,' said Mr. Spearman in wonderment. 'Who is it?'

There was a chuckle.

'I guess you don't know, eh?' The voice still shook with laughter. 'You're goin' to get a shock, I reckon. Listen, boy, this is the feller you spoke to at the fillin' station. Get me?'

Mr. Spearman started. He knew who it was now. Lefty Guinan.

'I get you,' he drawled. 'What do you want?'

'I want to see you,' answered Lefty. 'I want you to meet me at the end of the Wilshire Boulevard. I'll be waitin' with a car — '

'Nothing doing,' broke in Mr. Spearman. 'Think I'm one of those people who are born every minute?'

'I guess you will be one if you don't,' said Guinan, and there was a snarl in his voice. 'Say, listen, I've been havin' a chat with your sweetie, Mary Henley. She's with us now, and she's not feelin' kinda comfortable without you.'

Mr. Spearman's hand clenched hard on the vulcanite of the black cylinder he was holding to his ear, and his face was perceptibly whiter.

'What's the idea?' he demanded hoarsely.

'I guess you've got somethin' of mine,' said Lefty Guinan. 'You bring it with you and then you can see Miss Henley home.'

There was a little silence. Nothing had been said in so many words, but Mr. Spearman understood the threat that lay under the apparently innocuous words. Guinan had in some way got hold of Mary and was holding her as a hostage in exchange for the film and the money. His guarded way of saying so was, of course, due to the fact that the hotel operator might be listening in.

'All right,' Mr. Spearman said, suddenly making up his mind. 'I'll meet you.'

'Sure, that's fine!' answered Guinan. 'Don't forget to bring those things with you.'

There was a click as he rang off. Tommy Spearman wiped the perspiration off his forehead. The greater part of the money he could take, but the film — that was beyond his reach now.

He flung off his dressing gown, put on his jacket, and struggled into an overcoat. Hesitating for a moment, he went to his bedroom and came back with an automatic which he slipped in his pocket. Rivington had overlooked that when he searched the suite, for the simple reason that Mr. Spearman had put it on the windowsill of the adjoining suite which was empty and which he could reach from his own window.

The lift took him down to the vestibule, and he nodded to the night porter as he passed out. The broad boulevard was practically deserted as he walked swiftly along, but if it had been crowded Mr. Spearman would not have noticed the difference. He saw the car standing beside the sidewalk, and as he came up Lefty Guinan got out.

'Glad to see you, Tommy,' he said with an unpleasant grin. 'Brought that film?'

'No,' said Mr. Spearman, 'I haven't, for the reason that I haven't got it. What have you done to that girl, Guinan?'

'Nothin' yet,' snarled Lefty Guinan, 'but unless I get the money and the film somethin's goin' to happen to her. You can bet your sweet life.'

'What have you done with her?' demanded Mr. Spearman.

'Sure, she's safe enough,' was the retort, 'and if you do as you're told she'll be OK.'

'Do you think I'm going to take your word that she's all right?' snapped Mr. Spearman, and his voice was hard. 'See here, Guinan, you take me to her at once and I'll talk business. But I'm not doing anything until I've seen her.'

'That's OK with me,' said Lefty. 'Get in.'

'You get in first,' grunted Mr. Spearman, and the automatic glinted in the car's dim lights. 'Don't forget that I've got this!'

Lefty Guinan got into the car, and Mr. Spearman followed him. They were both too engrossed in their own business to see the figure that slipped out of the shadows of the sidewalk and perched itself on the back of the car as it moved off.

17

Guinan Shows His Teeth

The car, with Lefty at the wheel, ran on through the night. Every now and again the driver cast a sidelong glance at the silent figure seated next to him, and his lips twitched. Mr. Spearman sat rigid, his gun resting on his knees, the muzzle pointing towards the man beside him. This was not quite as Mr. Guinan had planned, and as each revolution of the wheels took them nearer to their destination his brain worked rapidly to find a means of steering things in the way he wanted them to go. That unpleasant pistol, with its menacing muzzle, must be got rid of. While Tommy Spearman held that he also held the whip hand. Lefty drove on, his brows drawn together in a frown that was not entirely due to concentration on his driving.

'How much farther have we to go?'

asked Mr. Spearman suddenly.

'Gettin' impatient?' growled Lefty.

'Naturally,' answered the other calmly. 'I want to get this business over and done with.'

'Sure! So do I,' snarled Guinan. 'I want that money and I want the film.'

'I think it's very doubtful whether you'll get either,' retorted Tommy Spearman, 'but if you've done any harm to the girl you'll get something that you won't like. I can promise you that.'

Lefty Guinan showed his teeth.

'Gettin' all high-hatted, aren't you?' he muttered. 'Anybody 'ud think you were goin' to do the bargainin' — '

'Anybody would be right,' answered Mr. Spearman, 'Just get that into your head, Lefty. At the present moment I'm in the position to dictate terms, not you. I've only got to press my finger on this trigger and you'd cease to exist. Keep that clearly before you — it'll save a lot of trouble.'

Lefty Guinan made no reply. It was just that fact that was worrying him. By now they had left the last of the streets of

Culver City behind them and were running through open country. It was too dark for Mr. Spearman to be able to see where they were, although he strained his eyes into the darkness ahead, for he was intensely curious to learn their destination. Presently the car pulled up with a jerk.

'Here we are,' said Lefty, and he made a movement to get out.

'Don't move,' ordered Mr. Spearman gently. 'I'll get out first, Lefty, if you don't mind.'

Guinan muttered an oath, but he was helpless, and watched his companion get slowly and cautiously out of the car, keeping him covered all the while with the snub nose of the automatic.

'Now you can get out,' said Mr. Spearman pleasantly, when he stood in the roadway, and Lefty obeyed. 'Which way do we go?'

'This way,' growled Guinan, choking back his rage.

He led the way over to the rickety gate and passed through into the weed-choked path leading up to the house. Tommy

Spearman followed him interestedly.

'So this is your rural retreat, is it?' he remarked when they came in sight of the house. 'Very pleasant, Lefty. Is this the place where you've brought Miss Henley?'

'This is the place,' grunted Guinan. 'Why don't you put that pistol away, Tommy, and let's talk things over comfortably?'

Mr. Spearman smiled.

'I'm quite comfortable as things are, Lefty,' he answered, 'and I've got an idea that if I hadn't got this pistol I shouldn't be! Go on; don't stop! I want to see the inside of this desirable residence.'

Lefty went round to the broken French windows and stepped inside.

'Where's the admirable Spike?' asked Mr. Spearman as they crossed the empty room. 'Surely he's about somewhere?'

'Sure he's about somewhere,' snapped Lefty. 'He's at the back with the girl.'

He negotiated the passage that led to the kitchen and opened the door. Spike Munro, who was sitting on a box chewing stolidly at his inevitable gum, looked up.

'Got him?' he asked quickly.

With the muzzle of his pistol Tommy

Spearman pushed Lefty Guinan further into the room.

'Good evening, Spike,' he said genially. 'Or rather, good morning. You haven't cured yourself of that horrible vice of chewing yet, I see.'

Spike uttered an oath and sprang to his feet, and instantly Mr. Spearman's voice became stern.

'Don't move, Spike,' he said sharply. 'I hate violence in any form, but if you don't keep still I shall, without hesitation, shoot you. I mean that!'

The expression on Mr. Munro's face showed that he realised that this was no empty threat. His jaw dropped and he stared from the pistol in Mr. Spearman's hand to Lefty Guinan and back again.

'I guess you'd better do what he says, Spike,' muttered Guinan. 'He's got the drop on us.'

'A most sensible remark,' said Mr. Spearman. 'Go over and join your friend. The farther away from me you are the better I like it. That's right,' he went on as Lefty Guinan slouched sullenly over to Spike's side. 'Now let's get to business.'

187

Without moving from the doorway he glanced quickly round the kitchen lit by the dim light of two candles. His eyes met those of Mary and he smiled.

'Don't be frightened, Miss Henley,' he said encouragingly. 'You'll soon be free.

He had heard the little exclamation of surprise and pleasure she had uttered at the first sound of his voice, but his attention had been too occupied then with Guinan and Spike Munro.

'How — how did you know what had happened to me?' she asked in surprise.

'I didn't, until our mutual acquaintance over there — ' He nodded towards Lefty Guinan. ' — told me.'

'But I don't understand.' She frowned in perplexity. 'Why should he have told you?'

'I'm afraid,' said Tommy Spearman, 'that the explanation at the moment would take too long. At the present time I'm anxious to get away from here, and I'm sure you are too.'

He had kept one eye on Spike and Lefty during this short conversation, and now he said, addressing Guinan:

'Untie her, will you?'

'See here, Spearman,' began Spike; but Lefty, a little gleam in his eyes, interrupted him.

'Shut up!' he said gruffly, and going over to where the girl lay, pulled a knife from his pocket and slashed through the cords that bound her.

'Now — ' said Mr. Spearman, and that was all he said, for with a sudden movement that took him completely by surprise Lefty Guinan lifted the girl so that her body came between him and the pistol that was covering him.

In the same movement the knife which he had used to cut her cords swung up until its sharp point pricked her throat.

'Now — what?' asked Lefty Guinan triumphantly. 'I guess that if you attempt to shoot me you'll hit the girl, and if you fire at Spike I'll cut her throat!'

Mr. Spearman stood motionless, but his face had gone suddenly white. Lefty saw the effect of his words and gave a short laugh.

'Not so confident now, are you, Tommy?' he sneered. 'Not so darned clever as you thought you were, eh?'

'If you touch that girl — ' began Tommy Spearman.

'I guess I shan't touch her, so long as you do as you're told,' broke in Guinan. 'Spike, go and take his gun.'

Spike hesitated,

'Go on! He daren't hurt you!' snapped Lefty. 'If he tries any funny business this knife goes into the girl's throat.'

Spike Munro came over, and with a shrug of his shoulders Mr. Spearman gave up his pistol and thrust his hands into his pockets.

'You win,' he said unemotionally. 'What happens next?'

'You'll see!' Lefty Guinan could not keep the note of exultation from his voice, 'I guess you'll see what happens next, Tommy. Get some more of that rope, Spike, and truss him up.'

Mary Henley, her eyes wide with fear, watched while Spike Munro went over to the corner and came back with a hank of cord, part of which had already been used to tie her. With this he proceeded to secure Mr. Spearman's wrists and ankles.

Spearman made no effort to resist. He realised that any show of fight on his part would result in injury — probably death — to the girl. He accepted his defeat with the nonchalance of the born gambler. His brain was busy all the same, and even while Spike was tying him up he was striving to evolve some means of getting out of this unpleasant position.

'Now, come on, fix up the jane again,' ordered Lefty Guinan when Spike had finished and Tommy Spearman lay helpless. 'I'll hold her while you do it.'

Ten seconds later Mary was once more securely bound.

'Now, who's going to dictate terms?' said Lefty, smiling unpleasantly.

'You are, I presume,' retorted Mr. Spearman, looking at him steadily. 'And for heaven's sake be quick about it. I'm most uncomfortable!'

Lefty lit a cigarette.

'Not so uncomfortable as you will be, Tommy,' he said. 'I guess I want two things from you — that money you stole from me and the film,

'I don't see how you're going to get

either while you keep me tied up,' said Tommy Spearman calmly. 'But I'll tell you what I will do. Release Miss Henley and let her go and I'll give you half the money.'

Guinan laughed.

'What do you take me for?' he asked. 'A kid? I want all that money and I'm going to have it!'

'The difficulty about that,' said Tommy Spearman, 'is that the money is at my hotel.'

'Sure that will be easy,' said Lefty. 'I'll come back with you and get it. Spike can stop here with the jane, and if I'm not back in a couple of hours — well, it won't be pleasant for her.'

'Nothing doing, Lefty,' said Spearman, shaking his head. 'You've got to let that girl go before I do anything.'

'Don't talk soft.' snapped Guinan impatiently. 'Do you think I was born yesterday? The girl's the only hold I've got on you. Once I let her go, you can snap your fingers at us. I know that as well as you do — '

'Listen, Lefty,' Mr. Spearman spoke

earnestly, 'this business is between you and me. Miss Henley's got nothing whatever to do with it. Let her go, and I'll give you my promise that you shall have your money.'

'And the film?'

'And the film,' agreed Mr. Spearman.

'Oh, yeah? You think I'm goin' to fall for that stuff,' said Lefty, 'Your promise! I guess that means just nothin' to me. When the money and the film are in my hands I'll think about lettin' the girl go, but not before.'

'Until she's safe you won't get them, Lefty,' said the other decidedly. 'And you can't get them without me, remember that, so you'd better agree to my terms.'

'I'm not goin' to try and get them without you,' snarled Guinan savagely, 'and I'm not goin' to talk to you all night. For the last time, will you come with me to your hotel and get that money and the film?'

'The film isn't at my hotel,' answered Mr. Spearman.

'Where is it?' demanded Guinan.

'It's quite safe,' said Tommy Spearman.

'Well, wherever it is, I guess you can get it,' grunted Guinan.

'Oh, I can get it all right,' answered Mr. Spearman, 'and I will — on the terms I have stated.'

'You'll get it on mine,' snapped Guinan, 'and the money as well. Is the film at your hotel?'

'No, it's not!' snapped Spearman shortly.

'Where is it?'

'That's my business,' retorted Mr. Spearman.

Lefty Guinan's face became contorted with rage, and stooping, he struck his captive full in the face. The blow was a heavy one, and cut Tommy Spearman's lips so that the blood trickled down his chin.

'That's the sort of thing I should have expected from you,' he said quietly, but there was that in his tone which lashed Lefty to fury.

'Never mind what you expected,' he hissed thickly. 'I guess that's only a taster of what's coming to you unless you do what you're told, so you'd better listen.

I've changed my plan. What you'll do is to tell us where the film is and write a note to your hotel authorising the bearer to collect some things from your room. Spike can take that along, and when he comes back with the money and the film you and the girl can go — see?'

'I hear,' corrected Mr. Spearman, 'and I'll see you in hell first.'

'Very well.' Lefty was almost incoherent with fury. 'P'raps this'll make you alter your mind.'

He strode over to the mantelpiece, seized one of the candles and stooped over Mary Henley.

'Now,' he snarled, and his lips were drawn back showing his yellow teeth, 'you'll do what I want or I'll burn the girl until she screams!'

He brought the flame of the candle to within an inch of her hand.

'Come on! I guess I'll give you two seconds to make up your mind!'

16

Bob Rivington Finds Trouble

Bob Rivington had been watching the Beverley Wilshire for a long time before he was rewarded by any concrete result. He had seen Mr. Spearman go to his dinner at the Brown Derby and had seen him come back again, although he had kept so well hidden himself that Mr. Spearman had not spotted him.

After that had followed a long and tedious wait, during which Bob had become thoroughly and wholeheartedly bored. But he stuck to his post, and later was glad that he did. Just as he was looking about for the arrival of Paul, who had promised to relieve him, Mr. Spearman came out again and began walking up the Wilshire Boulevard at a great pace. Bob, with a thrill of interest, followed him. This looked as if there was something doing at last. It was unlikely that Mr. Spearman was merely going out for a breather; everything about him showed purpose and decision.

Bob forgot his boredom in the sudden keen excitement that came over him. He quickly found that shadowing his quarry was going to be easy, for the man he was following seemed so intent on his business, whatever it was, that he never once looked back.

Bob began to speculate on where he was going. Paul's object on having a watch kept on the Beverley Wilshire was his belief that in spite of the fiasco of his search, the million-dollar film was somewhere in Mr. Spearman's possession, and that sooner or later he would make a move to shift it to a less dangerous resting place.

Well, wherever the con man was going on this night excursion he was not taking the film with him. He was carrying nothing — at least nothing so bulky as that. Bob was intensely curious, and presently his curiosity was satisfied, for at the end of the Boulevard he saw the dim lights of a stationary car. So that was it.

Mr. Spearman was going to meet somebody. Who?

He increased his pace, making no sound with his rubber-soled shoes, and keeping well in to the shadow of the sidewalk, edged as close as he could to the waiting car. Mr. Spearman came abreast of it and a man got out. Bob heard him say something. He wasn't close enough to hear what it was, but something in the tone of the man's voice was familiar. He moved a few paces nearer, and now he was able to hear Spearman's reply.

'What have you done with the girl, Guinan?'

Bob's pulses beat at double their normal speed, for the man in the car was Lefty Guinan — the man who had killed Levenstein. This was getting exciting! But who was the girl they were talking about? He strained his ears to hear some more, but the voices of the two had dropped, and he could only catch a word here and there — not sufficient to make sense of the conversation.

One thing, however, he thought rapidly, he must not let Guinan out of his sight, and that was going to be awkward, because the man had got a car. Wait a minute, though: the car was a two-seater with the hood up, and there was ample room on the back for a passenger — provided he could get there unobserved. Cautiously he crept nearer yet, and as he did so he heard Guinan say,

'That's OK with me. Get in.'

'You get in first,' answered Spearman, and Bob saw with a little thrill that he was holding an automatic pistol.

So this was not a friendly meeting! He watched them both get into the little car and saw it move forward. Breaking into a run he covered the small space that now separated him from the back of the car and perched himself on it as securely as he could. This was not quite as securely as he would have liked, for the jerk as it gathered speed almost unseated him and sent him rolling into the roadway. But by gripping the right wing and wedging his foot into the rear-lamp bracket he managed to retain his hold. The car ran at a fair speed, negotiating a maze of streets which were completely unfamiliar to Bob, and he soon lost all sense of his direction. He had not the faintest idea of their destination, but he hung on grimly with one resolve, and that was that wherever Guinan was going, he was going too.

Presently the streets were left behind, and rough roads and byways took their place. Several times as the car bumped over the bad surface Bob was nearly thrown from his precarious perch, and it was more by luck than anything else that he still stuck on. By the time the car came to a halt under the shadow of a wooded hillside he was bruised all over and aching in every limb. Immediately it stopped he slipped down and hid himself behind a clump of bushes that were growing close at hand. He saw Spearman get out, followed by Lefty Guinan. Talking in low tones, both of them moved over to a gate at the foot of the sloping hillside. Through this they both disappeared, and Bob waited to give them time to get well out of the way before he followed. The gate seemed to suggest there was a house somewhere close at hand. When he concluded that a sufficient time had elapsed he left his place of concealment and was moving towards the gate when an idea occurred to him, and he stopped by the car. Bob knew all about cars, and in a few seconds he had lifted the bonnet and cut three inches from each of the wires leading to the plugs. The car as a means of locomotion was now about as useful as a soapbox, and the fact that it was out of gear might prove useful later.

Having accomplished that little bit of forethought, Bob walked over to the gate and entered the dark lane beyond. It was very dark, and he could scarcely see a yard before him, owing to the trees, which grew so thickly that they obscured the sky.

He went on, however, for what must have been a good fifty yards, and then suddenly he came in sight of a house. He stopped and surveyed it, and came to the conclusion that it was the most depressing place he had ever seen.

Behind it and on either side a small forest hemmed it in, and in front was a riot of unkempt bushes and long grass. The house itself was low and rambling

201

and drifted away into the shadows that surrounded it. No gleam of light came from any of the broken windows and no sound broke the absolute stillness. Bob stood for a moment, taking in every detail of this unprepossessing building, and then he decided to have a closer look.

Wading knee-deep in tangled weeds and grass, he made his way towards a flight of broken steps that led to a veranda that ran almost the entire length of the front of the place. Mounting the crazy steps cautiously, he found that two pairs of French windows opened on to the balcony. He went to the first pair and found that they were open. He pulled them wider, and holding them thus, listened. He thought he heard the faint sound of voices, and stepped into the room beyond. The dust was thick everywhere, and as he walked forward it rose in clouds, and it struck him that the house must have been uninhabited for years. Again halfway across that dim room he paused and listened.

Yes, there was no mistaking this time; from somewhere inside the place — at the back probably — came the hum of voices. Bob frowned. He was sorry now that he had put the car out of action. What a chance he had missed! He could have gone back, fetched Paul, and rounded the whole crowd up. However, it was no good being sorry now.

He decided to go forward on his own. On tiptoe he crossed the remainder of the room, passed through an open door, and came out into a narrow passage. This seemed to run right and left, but the vague whispering which he had heard had grown louder, and came from the left. He started to feel his way along, and almost came to grief over a short flight of steps that led downwards. Ahead of him was a door, and from underneath came a thin stream of light. Very carefully he approached it, and bending down, applied his eye to the keyhole. He shifted his position until he could get a clear view of the room beyond, and the sight that he saw made him draw in his breath quickly. The room had evidently been a kitchen and was lit by two candles stuck on the end of the mantelpiece. And in this feeble glimmer he saw that there were four people present — three men and a girl. Spearman was lying securely bound in one corner, and in the other — bound too — was the girl with whom he had come into the Brown Derby. But Bob had only eyes for what Lefty Guinan was doing, for as he watched he took one of the candles from the mantelpiece and went over to the girl.

'Now,' he snarled, bending over her, 'you'll do what I want or I'll burn the girl until she screams. Come on! I'll give you two seconds to make up your mind!'

Bob saw the flame of the candle approach the girl's hand, and heard Spearman cry:

'You brute! Stop — '

And then pulling his automatic from his pocket, he threw discretion to the winds and flung open the door.

'Drop that candle!' he said crisply, 'and put your hands up! I want you!'

With a growl of surprise like that of a wild beast, Lefty dropped the candle and stood up.

'Put your hands up!' repeated Bob, 'and look slippy or I'll — ' They never

204

heard what he was going to do, for at that moment Spike, who was close to the mantelpiece, swept the last remaining candle to the floor and plunged the place in darkness!

Bob's fingers contracted on the trigger of his gun, and the little weapon spat flame. He had to keep it high for fear of hitting Spearman or the girl. He heard a cry and a muttered oath, and guessed that either Guinan or Munro had been wounded. Then a hand gripped his wrist, and the pistol was wrenched from his grasp. He hit out blindly and his blow struck flesh, but his attacker reached up and gripped his throat. He tried with all his might to wrench that hand away, but the fingers only tightened and sank into his flesh. He kicked out and felt his foot strike home. There was a grunt of pain, but the grip never relaxed. There came a roaring in his ears, and flecks of red danced in the darkness that was like a wall shutting him in. He flung himself backwards and fell heavily with his assailant on top of him. Bunching his fist he struck out with all his strength. The grip on his throat relaxed, and with great panting gulps he drew air down into his bursting lungs. But the respite was only short-lived. He heard a growled-out oath, and something crashed down on his head. He gave a stifled groan and then all the darkness in the world seemed to rush into his brain . . .

19

Shots in the Night

Paul Rivington was feeling irritable. He had been morose during dinner, and directly after the meal had betaken himself to the room that Mr. Myers had set aside for his exclusive use, and drawing up a chair to the open window, smoked cigarette after cigarette, staring unseeingly out into the fragrant darkness of the garden.

He had come at the frantic request of Elmer Myers six thousand miles and he had succeeded in doing comparatively nothing. And so far as he could see might continue to do nothing unless his hunch that Tommy Spearman was the possessor of the million-dollar film was right. If Tommy had the film he was bound to try and dispose of it, and it was then that Paul hoped to catch him. And he felt pretty sure that he had got it somewhere.

The fact that he had failed to find it at the Beverley Wilshire meant nothing.

Spearman was a clever man and might have hidden it anywhere in the hotel. One thing, however: so long as a close watch was kept on his movements he would not be able to shift it. The whole case was very unsatisfactory. One of the most difficult he had ever had to deal with, because there were so many cross currents. This murder, for instance, of Lamont. Who had done that? Clearly not Lefty Guinan and his accomplice, Spike Munro, for, if so, there would have been no need for Dick Rennit to take the blame. And that Rennit had not committed it himself, Paul was almost sure. His confession was too vague regarding details; he could not say, for instance, what he had done with the weapon. No gun had been found on the scene of the crime, and Rennit, when questioned, had said that he'd thrown it away when he had left the studios, but a search had not brought it to light. No, Rennit had confessed to the murder in order to shield somebody, and that somebody could only be the girl, Mary Henley. At least that was Paul's theory, and Mary Henley was apparently a close friend of Tommy Spearman. Was the girl guilty, and if so, what had been her motive? Had she been one of the people who had burgled the studios that night? Again, why should she?

Surely crooks like Guinan and Spike Munro wouldn't take a girl along with them on that sort of business. The whole thing was a mix-up, and the more Paul thought of it the more of a mix-up it became. It was with something very like relief that he rose at last and prepared to go down to the Beverley Wilshire to take Bob's place. That was the only line they had got at present — Tommy Spearman. He was in it up to the neck, and he might eventually lead them to the truth.

As he left the gate of Myers's house a big car that was passing stopped with a squeal of brakes, and as he drew level with it Captain Willing thrust his head through the window.

'Hello, Mr. Rivington!' he called. 'I thought it was you. I guess we've found out where those two birds, Guinan and Munro, were staying.'

'Good!' said the detective. 'Did you find anything to tell where they'd gone?' Captain Willing made a grimace.

'No,' he answered, 'they've left a lot of stuff behind, though, which proves that they were the fellows who did the job at Mammoth Studios. We've found a complete outfit of burglar's tools — gas cylinders and everything.'

'Where were they staying?' asked Paul.

'At Mack's,' replied Willing. 'It's a second-rate hotel on the way to Los Angeles. We've just been round combing the apartment houses to see if we can find any trace of them. Where are you going? Can I give you a lift?'

Paul told him where he was going.

'Jump in,' said Willing. 'We're going past there. We'll drop you.'

He opened the door and the detective got in.

'Do you still think Spearman's got that film?' asked Willing as the car moved off.

'I do,' answered Paul. 'I'm sure he has.'

'Why not give him a surprise visit, and

have another look?' the other suggested, but Paul shook his head.

'Because I don't think it would do any good,' he replied. 'Tommy Spearman's clever, and I don't think we should find anything. All we can do — ' He broke off and sat forward.

A small car had just gone by, travelling at fair speed, and as the light of the police car caught the rear he saw with surprise that a figure was crouching precariously on the back. For one fleeting second he saw the rider's face and recognised his brother.

'What's the matter?' asked Willing, astonished at his companion's sudden alertness.

'That car that's just gone by, did you see it?' said Paul.

Willing nodded.

'Yes, carrying an extra passenger in the back,' he said. 'The way they crowd these small cars — '

'That passenger was my brother,' broke in Paul. 'Tell your driver to keep that car in sight.'

'Your brother?' Willing's jaw dropped,

and without much more ado he reached forward and jerked aside the glass panel in the window that separated them from the driver's seat. 'See that car — that car that's just gone by?' he said, and the driver nodded. 'Keep it in sight — don't get too near. Follow the tail-light.'

'And tell him to put our headlights out,' said Paul. 'There's something in this, Willing. Bob's after someone in that car, and we don't want to let them know we're following.'

Willing nodded and gave the additional order. The headlights went out, they sped along in darkness and practically in silence. The red tail-light of the car they were trailing twinkled ahead, a small star of light in the blackness of the night. It twisted and turned down one street after another, and Captain Willing whistled.

'Where the hell are they going?' he muttered. 'We shall be out in the country in a minute.'

'I don't know where they're going,' said Paul, 'but wherever it is, we're going too. Bob must be following Spearman.'

'Well, I guess it looks as if we are in for

some joy-ride,' said Willing. 'That's the last of Culver City.'

The houses and shops and streets had frayed out into hedges and wooded hillside, but the star point of red light kept steadily on — and then came disaster, swift and sudden. The engine of the police car gave a preliminary cough, spat spasmodically twice, and then — stopped.

'What's the matter?' asked Willing, pushing back the panel quickly.

'Gas,' said the driver laconically. 'I guess we've run out.'

Willing uttered an oath.

'Haven't we a spare can?' he said.

'No, sir,' was the reply. 'I didn't know we were going so far. I relied on being able to fill her up at a filling station.'

'What do we do now?' asked Willing blankly,

Paul opened the door and dropped into the roadway. The red tail-light of the car they were pursuing had vanished.

'Go on foot,' he said.

'Do you know this road?'

'Yes,' said Willing.

'Where does it lead to?'

'Down to the coast eventually,' was the reply. 'But they can't be going there.'

'Any houses?' asked the other, and Willing shook his head.

'No,' he replied, and then: 'Yes there is, though. One. The haunted house.'

'What do you mean?' said Paul sharply.

'There's a house, or rather the remains of one, about a mile and a half farther along,' said Willing. 'It used to belong to a film director — a Russian. He shot himself, and after that nobody would take the place. It's nearly falling to pieces.'

'Perhaps that's where they're making for,' said Paul. 'Anyway, we may as well follow and see if we can pick up the car. Are you coming?'

'Sure!' said Willing.

He spoke to the driver, and then he and Paul set off side by side. They seemed to have been walking for hours when rounding a bend they suddenly came upon the car. It was standing motionless, and without lights, drawn into the side of the road.

'I believe you're right, Mr. Rivington,' whispered Willing excitedly. 'Whoever was in the car has gone to the house I spoke of. Anyway, there's the gate.'

He pointed to a dilapidated gate hanging from one hinge and standing half open.

'I — ' began Paul Rivington and stopped.

From beyond the gate, muffled but distinct in the stillness of the night, came the sound of two shots!

20

Mr. Spearman Justifies His Existence

Mr. Spearman lying bound and helpless in the dark, with the struggle going on around him, wondered who was winning. He was soon to know, for as suddenly as the fight had started it ended, and Lefty's voice, hoarse and breathless, called out in the blackness:

'Spike! Spike, darn you! Find a candle, can't you?'

A grunt answered him.

'There ain't no more,' said the plaintive voice of Spike Munro. 'Those two were the last.'

Guinan uttered an oath.

'You fool!' he snarled. 'Why didn't you get more?'

'Sure, I thought there'd be enough,' protested Spike.

'Well, find a light of some sort,' snapped Guinan, 'and be quick. One of that swab's bullets got me in the arm and it's hurting like blazes.'

'I ain't got no matches,' said Spike. 'Where's your lighter?'

'I left it in the car,' said Guinan. 'Go down and get it. There's a cupboard on the dashboard.'

Spike Munro grumbled something in reply and Mr. Spearman heard him stumble across the room and then go out. There was a pause, and then Lefty uttered an exclamation and came over to where Spearman was lying.

'Say, have you got any matches?' he muttered, feeling about in the darkness until his hands touched the bound man.

'There's a lighter in my pocket,' said Spearman.

'Why the hell didn't you say so before and save Spike going all the way down to the car?' growled Guinan.

He felt about, found the pocket, and extracted the lighter. There was a click and a feeble blue-white flame broke the intense blackness. Shielding the light with one hand, Lefty searched about on the floor for the candle that Spike had knocked off the mantelpiece. He found it, and, lighting it, stuck it back again.

'That's better,' he grunted, and looked quickly about him.

Bob was lying motionless near the door, and Guinan went over and peered into his upturned face.

'You won't worry anybody for a bit,' he said callously.

He picked up the automatic that had fallen from Bob's grasp in the struggle. He was looking anxiously at a deep furrow scrawled across the back of his left hand, which was bleeding profusely, when there was a hurried footstep and Spike came in, his face full of fear.

'Lefty,' he said excitedly, 'there's two guys comin' up to the house!'

'What?' Under the stain of his disguise Lefty Guinan's face went white.

'I just caught sight of 'em as I was goin' down to the car,' went on Mr. Munro. 'They're cops, I think.'

'Can you see them from the balcony?' rapped Guinan, and Spike nodded.

'Wait here,' said the other quickly, and hurried out.

They heard his footsteps thudding along the passage and then die away. Mr. Spearman smiled. This was a night of excitement with a vengeance! When Bob had arrived he had guessed that he must have been following him. These others were in all probability Rivington and the police. Well, it looked as if Lefty and Spike were in for a rough time, and serve them right. Quickly he set to work again on the cords at his wrist. Ever since Spike had finished tying him up he had surreptitiously been trying to loosen his bonds, and he had practically succeeded. Spike was in an agony of apprehension, biting his nails and staring at the door. Suddenly he stiffened as there came a fusillade of shots from outside. They were answered by a volley of curses. Mary screamed, and Spike swung round on her.

'Shut up, you!' he cried. 'Shut up. Do you hear?'

His voice was cracked and menacing, and the girl choked back the screams that filled her throat. Three more shots, closer at hand, and then the sound of running feet on bare boards, and Lefty burst into the room.

'Quick, Spike!' he panted, 'shut the door and bolt it!'

He flung aside his smoking gun.

'Give me that gat you took from Spearman.'

Spike dragged the weapon from his pocket, and thrust it into the other's outstretched hand.

'Now the door!' snapped Guinan, and Munro leaped forward.

But he was too late; even as the heavy door swung a foot was thrust forward between the jamb and the edge.

'Get back both of you!' cried the voice of Paul Rivington. 'I'll shoot the first one that moves an eyelid!'

He gave the door a shove with his shoulder and sent it crashing back against the wall. He stepped across the threshold, followed by Captain Willing.

'Put up your hands!' he ordered sternly, and Spike's arms rose above his head.

'Now you,' went on the detective, turning to Lefty Guinan, but Guinan met his gaze with an evil grin.

Crouched back against the wall in the corner he covered the helpless form of Mary Henley with the automatic Spike had taken from Mr. Spearman.

'You daren't shoot!' he jeered, his lips curled back until they showed his gums. 'I guess if you do I'll fire at the girl. You may hit me, but she'll get hers first.'

Paul bit his lip. Lefty Guinan was speaking the truth. He could see it in the man's eyes, and by the set of his face.

'What good do you think that's going to do you?' he asked. 'You can't get away.'

'Can't I?' snarled the gangster. 'We'll see about that. If you get me I go to the chair, and I might as well die by a bullet as that. Put your guns down on that box over there, or, by Heck, I'll pull the trigger and send the girl to hell.'

'Don't be a fool,' began Captain Willing. 'You daren't do it — '

Guinan laughed — a mirthless, raucous laugh.

'Daren't I?' he cried. 'Put those guns down or I guess you'll see.'

Rivington frowned. What could they do? Unless they did as Guinan wanted the girl would die. There was no question about that. Guinan was cornered, and he was taking the one chance that presented itself. A chance that would either lead to safety or death.

'Quick!' snapped Lefty in a voice that was harsh and cracked with the strain he was undergoing. 'Put down those gats, or — '

'We can't do it,' said Captain Willing. 'Stop bluffing, and give in, We can't bargain with you.'

'I'm doing the bargaining,' retorted Guinan. 'And I'm not bluffin'! You'll see that unless you do as I say!'

'I'm afraid we shall have to give in,' muttered Paul. 'It will mean the girl's life if we don't.'

'We must risk that,' answered Willing grimly. 'That man's a murderer and a dangerous crook. I guess we can't allow him to get away.'

The perspiration was pouring down his forehead, and Paul knew that he was speaking in accordance with his duty. It was his duty to take Guinan at whatever sacrifice.

'I'm goin' to count three,' said Guinan, 'and if those rods are not on the box by the time I've finished, it's goodbye to the girl.' He began to count slowly: 'One — ' Paul took a step forward.

'Guinan, you'll do no good — '

'Two!' And then from behind them a lean slim figure leaped forward and flung itself between the levelled pistol and the helpless form of Mary Henley.

Lefty's finger tightened on the trigger and the ugly muzzle of the weapon belched flame and lead. Thomas Spearman took three of the bullets in his chest before he succeeded in wrenching the pistol from Guinan's hand. They tore through clothing and flesh and muscle — three separate agonies of red-hot, searing pain, but there was a smile on his lips as he went down. Guinan turned with the snarl of a trapped animal, but Paul had already sprung forward and gripped him by the collar and wrist, and twisting his arm up behind his back, rendered him helpless in a ju-jitsu lock. A second later he was powerless to do further harm, with steel handcuffs locking his wrists behind his back. Rivington stooped down over the crumpled figure of Tommy Spearman.

'Glad you've — got — him, Rivington,' said Spearman faintly. 'I managed to — get free — while you were — all busy . . .'

His breath was coming with difficulty, and his face was twisted in pain.

'It was the — only thing — to do, wasn't it?'

'It was one of the bravest things I've ever seen,' said the detective sincerely.

Mr. Spearman smiled.

'Had — to — do it,' he muttered. 'I couldn't let — the girl . . .'

He broke into a fit of coughing, and with his handkerchief Paul wiped away the blood from his lips.

'Thanks,' said Spearman.

'You'll find — that film — at Los Angeles Post Office — John Clayton . . .'

A spasm of pain racked him, but he contrived to smile.

'Rivington —' Paul had to bend closer to catch the words at all, they were so faint. ' — you might tell — Mary —'

What he wanted to tell Mary Paul

never knew, for in that second of time the soul that was Thomas Spearman went back whence it had come, and the body that had been Thomas Spearman lay very still.

21

The Ultimatum

Mr. Elmer Myers woke early with a vague feeling of depression, and it was not until he was fully awake that he succeeded in tracing this indefinite sensation to its tangible cause. For the few hours that he had been asleep the matter of the film had been forgotten, and now as his senses came back to normal the worry of the past week swept over him like a flood. He rose feeling unrefreshed and tired, and a bath and a shave did little to counteract this weariness. His normal breakfast hour was seven-thirty. He was an energetic man, and believed in early rising. It was one of his maxims that a man could get through more work in the morning than at any other time of the day. The brain was at its brightest and freshest, and the body revitalised by sleep. This morning, however, Mr. Myers felt neither bright nor fresh as he came downstairs to his dining room.

Breakfast, as usual, was laid on the balcony, and crossing the big room, Elmer Myers took his place at a small table which stood in the shade of a flowering creeper. His newspapers were laid beside his plate, but the morning mail had not yet arrived. The film magnate was in no mood for news, and pushed them rather irritably aside as his butler approached with coffee.

'Good morning, sir,' said the man, as he put the tray down and began to pour out the coffee.

'Good morning,' grunted Mr. Myers. 'I guess I'll just have some grapefruit and fish this morning.'

'Nothing else, sir?' asked the butler.

Elmer Myers shook his head.

'No, thank you, nothing else,' he replied.

The butler disappeared into the house, and gulping down half a cup of coffee, Mr. Myers stared out over the green of the lawn. The morning was beautiful. The sun cast long golden yellow rays across the ground. There was a chorus of birds in the trees, behind which the leaves rustled softly, forming a running accompaniment to their trebles. But Mr. Myers neither saw nor heard anything of this.

His mind was completely occupied with the urgent necessity of doing something. The whole future of Mammoth Pictures, which incidentally included the future of Mr. Myers himself, hung in the balance. And the balance was slowly descending against him. If Paul Rivington succeeded in finding the film, then everything would be all right, but if he didn't, nothing could prevent a crash, and a pretty serious crash at that.

The whole business of Mammoth Pictures, which Mr. Myers with so much thought and care had laboriously built up, would fall in ruins about his ears, and he, himself, would be buried under the debris. Once this happened, it would be the finish. He would never be able to extricate himself from the resultant financial catastrophe.

He ate the grapefruit that was brought him slowly and deliberately, but the fish which followed he scarcely touched. After picking at it for a moment or two he pushed the plate aside, poured himself out another cup of coffee, and lit a cigar. He had barely savoured the first preliminary puff when the butler brought his letters.

There was quite a pile of them, and ripping them open, Myers carried out his usual procedure of skimming them through and putting the more important ones aside for future attention. This morning, although there were so many, there were few of any importance. Only three were spread out on the right-hand side of his plate, and then he opened the last letter.

At the sight of the envelope his frown had deepened, and as he read the contents it grew deeper still. The letter was from the bank which had found the greater part of the money for the film, and it was disconcerting. Myers read it twice, and the lines about his mouth became accentuated.

American Consolidated
Bank Inc.

August 10th.

Mr. Elmer Myers
The Ronda,
Beverley Hills.

Dear Sir,
My attention has been called to the fact that several rumours are going about regarding the film entitled *The Man-God*, which your corporation has recently completed and which was partly financed by us. The rumours are to the effect that the negative of this film is no longer in your possession, and that in reality it was stolen on the night that your film editor and cutter, Mr. Perry Lamont, was murdered. Whether these rumours are correct or not I cannot, of course, pass an opinion, but they are very disquieting and disconcerting, and my firm is not unnaturally both worried and anxious. They have instructed me to make an inquiry into the matter, and so I shall take the pleasure of calling on you at your offices at eleven o'clock on Wednesday morning, the 11th inst. I

shall be very glad if you will make it convenient to see me then.

Yours truly,
Elworth T. Rodd,
Branch Manager.

Mr. Myers read the letter again slowly for the third time, laid it down and chewed thoughtfully at the end of his cigar. So the fact that the film had been stolen had leaked out. It was, of course, bound to have happened, but Mr. Myers hoped that it would not have happened quite so soon. The question was: What was he going to say to this man who was calling on him in about three hours' time?

If he admitted the fact that the film had been stolen he might as well cut his own throat. On the other hand, it would be very difficult to stall Rodd convincingly. He was a shrewd man of business, and would take a lot of bluffing. For a quarter of an hour Mr. Myers thought hard, then picking up the letter he rose to his feet and went into the house. In the hall he found a maid and stopped her just as she was mounting the staircase.

'Mr. Rivington up yet?' he asked.

'I don't know, sir,' answered the girl. 'You gave instructions that Mr. Rivington wasn't to be disturbed until he rang.'

'Yes, I remember,' Elmer Myers said, nodding absently.

The girl looked at him and waited. Seeing that Mr. Myers had apparently forgotten her existence, she rather awkwardly turned and continued her way upstairs. He stood for a moment or two in the middle of the hall, pinching his lower lip, and then suddenly coming to a decision he walked over to the staircase and began to ascend the stairs in the wake of the girl.

Reaching Paul's door, he knocked, but there was no sound from within, and after a second or two he knocked again and louder. Still getting no reply, he turned the handle softly and opened the door. A glance showed him that the room was empty, and he frowned as he saw the bed had not even been slept in. He closed the door and paused irresolutely in the passage, then he went along to Bob's room and knocked there. The result was the same as Paul's. No answer. He opened this door, too, and peered in; as in the other case the room was empty and the bed smooth and undisturbed.

Mr. Myers reluctantly made his way downstairs again. Both Paul Rivington and his brother had obviously been out all night. Where had they been? Where were they at the present moment? A tiny spark of hope began to glow in Mr. Myers's breast. Perhaps Rivington had found something. Perhaps he was even now on the track of the stolen film. The stout managing director of Mammoth Pictures fervently hoped so.

Making his way to his study, he sat down at his desk and pulled the telephone towards him. Two seconds later he was talking to Frank Leyland. The young film director heard the news regarding the letter from the bank with genuine concern.

'What are you going to do about it?' he asked.

'What can I do?' said Mr. Myers helplessly. 'All I can hope to do is to put up a bluff. If I can talk to this guy, Rodd, convincingly enough, I may be able to satisfy him for the time being, and so be able to gain a respite. I don't know what Rivington's doing at the moment, but neither he nor his brother has been home all night, and there's just a chance they might be on to something. Anyhow, Frank, we can't hold out much longer. It's a question of hours now, not days. Unless we can get that film back there's going to be the biggest crash that Hollywood's ever seen.'

'What time's this fellow coming?' asked Leyland.

'Who — Rodd?' said Mr. Myers. 'He's made the appointment for eleven at the office.'

'Would you like me to be there?' said Frank.

'I guess that I'd like you to be in the building,' answered Elmer Myers, 'so that I can call you if necessary. But I think I'd better see this fellow alone first. If I could only feel that things were all right I could talk all right. The trouble is, I can't. I know that Rivington's doing his best — everybody's doing his best — but that isn't going to cut any ice with Rodd. I've got to be precious careful how I deal with him, Frank. I daren't tell him definitely that we've got the film, because if anything should happen and we don't get it, it's going to make it very awkward for me. On the other hand, I can't tell him that we haven't, because that would be like putting a match to a barrel of gunpowder.'

'It's a pretty nasty position for you,' said Leyland.

'Nasty,' said Mr. Myers feelingly. 'I'll say there ain't a word in the dictionary strong enough to describe it! I guess I'm dreading this interview more than I ever dreaded anything in my life.'

'I'm not surprised,' said Leyland sympathetically. 'Well, anything I can do, Elmer, you know I will.'

'That's swell of you, Frank,' replied Elmer Myers gratefully. 'But I don't think there's much you can do. Anyhow, I'll see you down at the office.'

He rang off and sat sucking his half-smoked cigar, which had gone out. He was completely unaware that it was no longer alight, and this, more than anything else, testified to the chaotic state of his mind. Presently he made a desultory effort to force his brain along other channels, and turned his attention to some other business which should have been occupying his full time. It was a feeble effort, but it served to partially fill the short period before it was time to order his car to drive him down to the building which housed the Mammoth Pictures Corporation Inc.

The timekeeper greeted him with cheery good morning and smiled, for everybody liked Mr. Myers, and none better than those who worked for him. He forced himself to reply as cheerfully as possible, and then made his way along to his office. It was a little after eleven when Mr. Elworth T. Rodd was announced.

'Shoot him in,' said Mr. Myers, and sat back with a heavy heart to await the coming interview,

Elworth T. Rodd was a tall man, and his height was accentuated by his extreme leanness. There were more visible bones in Mr. Rodd than were decent for a living human being. In fact he was nearly all bones. His skin was drawn tightly across his face, and his lips were so thin and bloodless that they scarcely existed at all. His hair was sparse and dry, and of a colour that was neither white nor grey, but a combination of both with a tinge of yellow. His eyes, sunk deep in his head, peered short-sightedly through a pair of enormous horn-rimmed spectacles, and his voice when he spoke was like the pattering of peas on tightly stretched parchment. He bowed to Mr. Myers and extended a thin hand.

'Good morning,' he said. 'Sorry I'm a little late.'

Mr. Myers waved him to a chair.

'Sit down,' he said, forcing himself to smile affably. 'Now, then, what's all this about, Rodd?'

Mr. Rodd coughed dryly and hitched up the knees of his trousers.

'I thought my letter was perfectly clear,' he answered, 'without any further explanation. Alarming rumours have reached me that there's something wrong with this film you've been making; that it has, to put it bluntly, been stolen.'

'How did these rumours reach you?'

237

asked Mr. Myers noncommittally.

The banker shrugged his shoulders and spread out his hands.

'How do rumours usually reach people?' he asked. 'We've heard it from various sources. I cannot tell you where it originated, but you'll realise that if it's true the position is a very serious one for us. We have sunk a considerable amount of money to finance the production of this picture, and from what you told me at the time the transaction was mooted, we had very little doubt of getting our money back. The film was a good commercial proposition, but if the negative has been stolen it means that our money has been lost, and we dislike losing money, Myers.'

'Who doesn't?' said Mr. Myers jovially. 'I think, Rodd, that the murder of Perry Lamont has led to a great deal of exaggeration. We have, I'll agree, held up the cutting of the picture, but we are negotiating with another editor, and I hope the delay will prove only a temporary one.'

'Then there's no truth in these rumours?' asked Mr. Rodd.

'So far as I'm aware,' said Elmer

Myers, smiling blandly, 'the film is perfectly safe.'

'I'm very glad to hear that,' answered the banker, and he made a strange grimace which was his way of smiling. 'I must say you've relieved my mind. You can assure me, then, that the film is still in your possession?'

'I can assure you,' said Mr. Myers carefully, 'that we shall have the film ready for its premier presentation on the date stipulated.'

'That is three weeks from now,' said the banker, and there was a pause. 'The vice-president of the bank,' he went on, 'is arriving from New York at two o'clock. I have been instructed to ask you to have the film ready for his inspection at four.'

Mr. Myers's inside felt as if he had suddenly consumed a large draught of lead. It was next door to impossible unless a miracle happened that he could recover possession of the film by then.

'I don't see how that can be done,' he answered, shaking his head. 'Lamont was in the middle of the picture when he was killed, and it's all in bits and pieces.

239

Sequences don't run consecutively.'

'That won't make any difference at all, Myers,' broke in Elworth Rodd. 'All the president wishes is to see for himself that these rumours are unfounded.'

'Well, I've told you — ' began Mr. Myers.

'Sure, I don't doubt your word,' the other interrupted him again, 'and the president doesn't either, but — ' He made a deprecating gesture. ' — it would be much more satisfactory to all concerned if some concrete proof were shown.'

'Surely,' said Mr. Myers a little indignantly, 'this is very unusual.'

'It is,' admitted the banker, 'but you will be the first to realise that this is an unusual position. You understand, Myers, the film is our security. I guess if we had advanced you money on shares we should be entitled to hold those shares, or at least to have proof of their existence. As a business man, you will be the first to appreciate this.'

'Sure, I see your point.' Mr. Myers could think of nothing else to say. After all, the bank was acting within its rights. It had advanced him a considerable sum of money, and the profits of the film had been the only security he had had to offer. The studio, the plant, and even his own house, the Ronda, were already heavily mortgaged. The bank had made little demur in advancing the money he required, but the banks in America are used to this kind of speculation, and regard it as part of their legitimate business. The greater part of the shares in Hollywood's enormous film industry are held by the banks. If the negative of the million-dollar film had been in his possession Elmer Myers would have agreed to the demand without hesitation. But in the circumstances — he racked his brains to think of a convincing reply.

Elworth Rodd saw his hesitation, and leaned forward.

'I'd advise you,' he said, speaking slowly and clearly, 'to have that film ready. I guess if it's not here for the president to see at four o'clock this afternoon the bank will demand an immediate repayment of the amount advanced to you.'

Mr. Myers moistened his lips.

'I — ' he began, and at that moment the telephone bell rang.

With something like relief at the respite, Mr. Myers reached out and lifted the receiver. With a word of apology to the banker he placed it to his ear and called into the mouthpiece.

'Hello!' he said. 'Yes, sure, this is Myers this end. Who's that? Rivington? Yes? Oh, yes.'

There was a long pause while his caller spoke rapidly over the wire, and the watchful Mr. Rodd saw an astonishing change come over the face of the managing director of Mammoth Pictures.

'Say, that's fine!' said Mr. Myers enthusiastically. 'Sure, I'll be right along — in about half an hour. Right, Rivington!'

He slammed down the telephone and turned to the banker. His face, which had looked so grey and lined, seemed suddenly to have filled out and become youthful.

'I guess you said four o'clock, Rodd, didn't you?' he remarked briskly.

Mr. Rodd nodded.

'OK!' said Elmer Myers. 'Bring the president of the bank along here at four o'clock, and I will have the film ready for you!'

22

An Unpleasant Shock

It was dawn before Captain Willington and Paul Rivington succeeded in getting Lefty and the now tearful Spike back to Los Angeles and safely locked up in a cell. After the death of Tommy Spearman they had secured them both and released the girl. While Paul and Bob waited at the empty house, Willing went back to where they had left the police car, carrying with him a can of petrol which he had found in the disabled car belonging to Lefty Guinan. By the time he came back with the car Bob, who had recovered consciousness just before he had left and had been a little groggy, was feeling better. Except for a lump that was nearly as big as an apple, where Guinan had hit him, and a racking headache, he was not very much hurt, and insisted on accompanying them back to Los Angeles, instead of being dropped on the way at Elmer Myers house, which Paul suggested.

Mary Henley, rather white and shaken with the effects of the ordeal which she had undergone, and the tragedy which had been so recently enacted in front of her eyes, accompanied them as far as her apartment, and when the sun rose over Beverley Hills, crimsoning the little white houses that nestled on their slopes, the house that had witnessed tragedy twice during its existence was left once more deserted save for the still figure that lay — Paul's handkerchief over its face — in the kitchen to await the coming of the ambulance.

'I'm glad we got 'em,' said Captain Benson when he had been routed out of his bed and told the news. 'Plucky of that guy, Spearman. Shows there's some good even in the worst of us.'

Paul agreed. He felt disinclined to discuss the passing of Tommy Spearman with Captain Benson at any great length. The ambulance was dispatched on its melancholy journey, and then a shorthand typist was sent for, and Paul's and Bob's statements were taken down, read over to them, and signed. This, together with the routine work in which they had to take part, occupied them for the best part of the morning. At a quarter past eleven, when they had come back from the cell with Benson, where they had unsuccessfully questioned the sullen Lefty Guinan, Paul put through a call to Elmer Myers's house.

He discovered that Myers had already left for his offices, and it was not until a quarter to twelve that he was able to find another opportunity of ringing that gentleman up. Mr. Myers, when he arrived at the detective bureau, was a different being from the harassed, gloomy-faced man whom Paul had dined with on the previous night. He shook hands with the detective eagerly and listened with interest while Rivington told him of what had occurred at the empty house on the hillside.

'Gee!' he exclaimed when the story was ended. 'It was durned brave of that fellow Spearman. So he had the picture all the time, did he?'

'Apparently,' answered Paul, 'and somehow or other he must have got it to the post office.'

'Let's go round and get it,' said Mr. Myers. 'I shan't feel completely comfortable until I've got the thing back in my hands.'

They left Bob at the police headquarters and drove round to the Central Post Office.

'I've come,' said Paul to the girl who came forward enquiringly, 'for a parcel addressed to John Clayton, which I believe was sent here to be called for.'

The girl pointed across the big room to a counter on the opposite side.

'Poste restante over there,' she said briefly.

Paul went 'over there', and repeated his enquiry. The clerk in charge, a platinum blonde, replaced the lipstick with which she had been adorning her appearance in her bag and condescended to give them her attention.

'What name did you say?' she asked.

'John Clayton,' repeated Paul.

She strolled over to a large rack and inspected a selection of parcels. In a few minutes she came back shaking her head.

'Nothing here for anyone of that name,' she said.

Rivington frowned.

'You're sure you haven't made a mistake?' he persisted.

The girl apparently took this as a personal affront, for her lips tightened and she said in a slightly louder tone:

'There ain't nothin' here for anyone with the name of Clayton.'

Paul felt a little nonplussed. Spearman had distinctly said Los Angeles Post Office, and he had concluded it was the Central one. There were others, of course, and the only thing to do was to try them all, since this had drawn a blank. He turned to Mr. Myers, whose face had assumed an anxious expression.

'Which is the next nearest from here?' he said.

'Maple Street,' answered Elmer Myers.

'Come on, then,' said Paul, 'we'll try there.'

They drove to Maple Street, but to their enquiry received the same answer as they got at the Central Post Office. Nothing had been received in the name of John Clayton. Beverley Avenue was equally as insistent. They came back to the waiting car, worried and anxious. The lines which had smoothed themselves out of Mr. Elmer Myers's fat face had come back.

'Say,' he said as they once more climbed into the car, 'I suppose this guy Spearman knew what he was talking about? He wasn't delirious or anything?'

Rivington shook his head.

'No, he knew what he was talking about,' he said. 'I can't understand it.'

'He wouldn't have been stringing you?' suggested the other.

'No, he was speaking the truth,' declared Paul emphatically, 'I'm certain of that.'

'Well, I guess we've tried every post office in the city,' said Elmer Myers, 'so what are we going to do now?'

'Go back to the Central,' said Paul briefly.

They went back to the Central, and Rivington asked to see the postmaster. After some little delay they were ushered into that official's office, and as clearly as possible the detective stated his business.

'I have reason to believe,' he said, 'that

a parcel was posted yesterday in this district, addressed to a Mr. John Clayton and probably to this post office. But I have enquired both at this building and the other post offices without being able to find any trace of it. Could you suggest what is likely to have happened to it?'

'Do you know where it was posted?' asked the postmaster.

'No, I'm sorry to say that I don't,' replied the detective.

'Or what time?' asked the other.

'No, I can't tell you the time either,' said Paul. 'But I should think it was sometime during yesterday afternoon or evening.'

'I guess if it was addressed to any of the post offices in this city,' said the postmaster, 'it would have arrived by now. If it had been posted yesterday afternoon it would have reached its destination last night. How is it addressed — 'To be left till called for'?'

'I believe so,' said Paul.

'Well, it ought to have arrived by now,' declared the postmaster. 'I'll call up and enquire.'

He picked up a telephone and spoke rapidly for a moment. Laying it back down, he looked up.

'The parcel department are going to see if they can trace it,' he said.

Paul thanked him and waited. In ten minutes a buzzer rang and the postmaster picked up the telephone again. For some time he listened, interjecting an occasional 'Yes' to the report that came over the wire. Then he turned to Paul with a shake of the head.

'No trace of it at all,' he said. 'They've been in touch with the post offices at Beverley Hills and in Culver City, and no parcel with that address had been handed in at any of them.'

Paul and Elmer Myers went back to the car.

'I guess it's a washout,' said Elmer Myers, 'and I've promised that guy, Rodd, to have it ready for him at four o'clock.'

Paul rubbed his chin in perplexity.

'I don't know what can have happened to it,' he confessed. 'Spearman must have posted it, or had it posted. Wait a minute, he must have had it posted. He couldn't have posted it himself because Bob was watching him, and if he'd come out with a bulky parcel such as the film would have been, Bob would have noticed it. So he must have got someone from the Beverley Wilshire to post it for him. I think our best move is go along there and make enquiries.'

Myers agreed rather dubiously. Although he would have clutched at a straw in his extremity, he was feeling so pessimistic that he had not very much hope of the result. The reception clerk at the Beverley Wilshire eyed them askance. The news of Mr. Spearman's death had already reached the hotel. The rooms he had occupied were in the hands of the police and the newspaper reporters were buzzing round like flies.

There was bound to be a pretty big scandal, and scandal is anathema to any hotel. It means the falling off in the number of guests, and in consequence a falling off in the amount of tips received by the staff. So that not only affects the management, but everybody employed.

The reception clerk, recognising Paul as the man who had accompanied Captain Willing on the first visit to Mr. Spearman, and holding him partly responsible for what had happened, was inclined to be ungracious. He listened, however to what the detective had to say, and promptly referred him to the manager. The manager was busy, and they had to wait a precious quarter of an hour before they succeeded in obtaining an interview with that august personage. When at last they did so he was inclined to be impatient and a little irritable.

'I guess you'd better see the porter,' he said. 'I can't help you. This is a dreadful business altogether. The reputation of the hotel is ruined.'

Paul was duly sympathetic, and went in search of the porter. The porter, who recognised Elmer Myers and had visions of a possible tip, was more amenable.

'Nope,' he said, 'I didn't take any parcels for Captain Chase, sir, and I don't think any of the bellboys did, or I should have seen them go out. Of course, one of them might have done so when I was attending to somethin' else. You'd better ask them.'

Paul asked them. He interviewed all the bellboys separately, but they all shook their heads and definitely stated that they had taken no parcels to the post for Captain Chase. Myers was in despair.

'It's no good, Rivington,' he said. 'Either Spearman didn't know what he was talking about or you misunderstood what he said.'

'I certainly didn't misunderstand what he said,' retorted Paul, 'and I'm convinced he knew what he was talking about. Somebody in this hotel posted that parcel — or rather was given it to post — and I'm going to find out who it was.'

He went back to the porter.

'Can I see the chambermaids who were on duty yesterday?' he asked. 'And anybody else whom Captain Chase could possibly have given that parcel to?'

The porter, whose visions of a tip had been amply justified, proceeded to make himself useful. He found the chambermaids and the valet, but their answers, as the others had been, were negative. Paul had almost given it up when one of the maids offered a suggestion.

'Williams might have taken it, sir,' she said.

'Who's Williams?' asked Paul quickly.

'Sure, he's the floor waiter, sir,' said the girl.

'Can I see him?' said the detective.

She shook her head.

'He hasn't come in yet today,' she answered.

'Why?' asked Paul.

'I don't know, sir,' she replied. 'He just hasn't come in.'

Paul went back to the worried manager.

'I want to find a man called Williams,' he said.

'He's ill,' answered the manager shortly. 'His wife rang up this morning to say that he had been taken ill last night. What with this scandal, and with being short-handed —'

Paul interrupted him.

'Will you give me the man's address?' he asked.

The manager not only could, but did. He gave it with an alacrity that suggested that he hoped by this means to get rid of them. And his hopes were justified in this direction, for as soon as Paul had got the address Paul took a hasty farewell of the harassed man and set off in search of Mr. Williams. As they got into the car Elmer Myers glanced at his watch.

'Half-past two, Rivington,' he said. 'We've got just an hour and a half to find that film!'

23

Still Missing

Mr. Williams lived in a small apartment house in a mean street in the lower part of the town. When Paul Rivington and Elmer Myers knocked on the door it was opened by a small thin woman, respectably dressed, who peered at them through a pair of steel-rimmed glasses.

'Mr. Williams live here?' asked Paul.

The woman nodded.

'Yeah,' she answered. 'He's in bed. He ain't well enough to see anybody. Are you from the hotel?'

'Well, yes, in a way I am,' replied the detective.

He didn't want to frighten this woman by telling her his real identity, and her rather natural mistake had offered a suggestion. 'I should like to see Mr. Williams for a few seconds if it's at all possible.'

'I guess it wouldn't do no good if you did see him,' said the woman. 'He's very bad; he was took queer on his way home last night. The doctor says it was a slight stroke. Is there anything I can do for you, sir?'

'Are you Mrs. Williams?' enquired Rivington.

'Sure that's me,' was the reply.

'Well, then, perhaps you can help us, Mrs. Williams,' Paul went on. 'I'm anxious to trace a parcel addressed to a Mr. John Clayton, and I thought it might be possible that it might have been entrusted to your husband to post.'

'Sure, sir, it was,' said the woman. 'It was brought home with him.'

Mr. Myers uttered an exclamation of delight.

'That's swell,' he breathed. 'Where is the parcel — have you got it?'

The woman shook her head.

'Nope, I haven't,' she answered.

'Where is it, then?' asked Myers sharply.

'Well, you see it was like this.' Mrs. Williams looked from one to the other.

'When John — that's my husband — was brought home queer, I guess I was so worried and everythin' was so upside-down that I forgot all about the parcel.' She paused.

'Yes, yes — go on,' said Paul.

'And I didn't remember it again,' the woman continued, 'until Nelly — that's our daughter — came home to lunch. She works just round the corner. She always has her meals at home. She drew my attention to it, and asked should she post it. I guess I thought that was the best thing she could do, so I give her the money, and she took it with her when she went back to work.'

'I see,' said Paul. 'Now which post office would she post it from?'

'Maple Street would be the nearest,' answered the woman.

'Thank you,' said the detective. He slipped a green-backed bill into the woman's hand. 'Please buy Mr. Williams some little delicacy with that,' he said, 'and I hope he'll soon be better.'

Mrs. Williams was effusive in her thanks, but Paul was in a hurry, so they had to cut her short and take their leave. Once more they went back to Maple Street, and there they met with a setback. The parcel addressed to John Clayton was there all right, but the postmaster emphatically declined to hand it over.

'Sorry,' he said politely but firmly, 'but I guess this parcel will have to be delivered in the usual way. It's addressed to the Central Post Office, and to the Central Post Office it's got to go.

Mr. Myers groaned.

'What time will it get there?' he asked.

'At a quarter after six,' answered the postal official.

'I must have it before four,' said Elmer Myers, turning helplessly to Paul.

'May I use your phone?' Paul put his question to the postmaster.

'Sure,' said that official, and indicated the instrument with a wave of his hand.

Rivington called the police bureau.

'Is Captain Benson there?' he asked. 'This is Paul Rivington this end. Put me on to him will you.' There was a short delay, and then he went on: 'That you, Benson?' he asked. 'Listen. Do something for me, will you?'

Rapidly he explained the situation, and when he had finished and received Captain Benson's reply he hung up the receiver and turned to the others.

'That's all right, Myers,' he said. 'Benson's sending a man down at once with an official order signed by the chief of the detective bureau to hand over the parcel to us.'

They had to wait for the man from headquarters to arrive, and never had waiting seemed so long. The seconds crept by while Elmer Myers fidgeted impatiently and kept glancing at his watch. At twenty minutes to four the man arrived with the order, and the parcel was handed over. Myers opened it eagerly and rapidly examined the contents of the seven black tin boxes it contained.

'I guess this is the film all right,' he said as he hastily did them up again. 'Come on, let's go and meet that darned bank president.'

They reached Mammoth Pictures Studios Inc. just as the hands of the clock over the facia pointed to four!

24

The Toast

'The only thing to find out now,' said Paul Rivington, 'is exactly how Lamont died.'

He was sitting in Captain Benson's office of the police bureau at Los Angeles an hour and a half after Mr. Elmer Myers had triumphantly produced the negative of the super-film for the benefit of the bank president.

'I expect that we shall find that Guinan did it,' said Benson, shrugging his shoulders. 'I guess he'll confess when we put him through it.'

'You've got nothing fresh out of Rennit, I suppose?' said the detective.

'No,' answered Benson. 'His attitude's a mystery to me. I don't think he did it, but he swears that he did, and gets all lit up if we don't appear to believe him.'

'To my mind his confession is the most

puzzling part of the whole thing,' said Paul. 'The only way to account for it — setting aside the obvious conclusion that he really did commit the crime himself — is as I said before, that he's shielding the girl. That means that he must have reason to believe that she did it.'

'Do you think she did?' asked Benson quickly.

'Candidly, I don't,' replied Paul, 'but I don't see any other explanation.'

'She may have done it,' said Benson thoughtfully. 'This guy Lamont was a nasty piece of work. If she did do it she probably had good cause.'

The telephone bell rang at his side and he picked up the receiver.

'Hello!' he called. 'Yeah, when was the discovery made? Just now, eh? H'm! OK, I'll send along at once.'

He put down the telephone and pressed a bell.

'Suicide,' he said briefly. 'A woman gassed herself.'

A patrolman came in answer to his summons.

'Tell Captain Hymer I want him, and get him to get in touch with the District Medical Officer. There's a suicide case.'

Paul watched and listened while he rattled off a stream of orders to Captain Hymer, who came in a minute after the patrolman had departed.

'The woman's name was Irene Claremont. She was a film extra, and she lived in an apartment in Cantor Street, 217a. Some people in the building smelt the gas and called the patrolman. He broke in the door and found her. Get along as quickly as you can; he's waitin' up there now.'

Paul started when he heard the address. It was the same as that at which they had dropped Mary Henley in the morning. The girl seemed to attract tragedy. Benson leaned back in his chair as Hymer took his departure.

'Well, that's another,' he remarked. 'I guess we've had a lot of suicides lately. These girls come to Hollywood from good jobs, thinking they've found El Dorado, and find that it's harder to get work here than any other city in the world. When their savings are spent there's nothing else left. Not that this particular jane was one of those; she was a regular. She did quite well for a long time, used to be one of Lamont's favourites. I suppose when he was bumped off the influence was gone, and she found it hard to get work.'

He was chatting to pass the time, rather than anything else, but Paul was rather interested.

'Did Lamont help a lot of girls?' he asked.

'Yes,' said Benson, and winked. 'He was always after any new girl who turned up, and when he got tired and attracted by another face he'd drop 'em like hot bricks. And that was the end of most of them. This dame, Claremont, though, lasted longer than any of the others. There was some talk of his marrying her at one time. I expect it was only talk — it doesn't sound like Lamont at all.'

He chatted on inconsequently, and Paul was on the point of leaving when the telephone bell rang again.

'Yes, Benson speaking,' said the captain. 'Oh, that you, Hymer? What is it?'

There was a pause and then Paul saw the other's face change.

'Hell!' he exclaimed, and then: 'Say, hold on a minute.' He turned to Paul. 'That woman Claremont killed Lamont,' he said. 'She's left a letter behind confessing, and the weapon with it, and there's one cartridge missing.'

Before Rivington could reply he was back at the phone.

'You fetch it along here with you as soon as you finish.' He slammed the receiver down and pressed a bell. 'So that was the jane that Rennit was shielding,' he said. 'I never knew there was anything between them. I thought he was sweet on this other one, Mary Henley.'

'So did I,' replied Paul, frowning. 'Did they know each other? I suppose they must have done, living at the same house.'

'We'll find out.' Benson looked up at the patrolman who entered. 'Have Rennit brought up here at once,' he ordered.

The man went away, and Paul looked across at the other.

'Ask them to bring Miss Henley, too,' he said.

Benson showed his surprise.

'Why?' he asked.

'I've got an idea,' said the detective.

'OK.' Benson picked up the telephone and gave the number of the apartment house. In two seconds he was talking to Hymer. 'Get someone to bring Miss Henley back here,' he ordered, 'and send that suicide letter along here, too.' He looked at Paul. 'She's coming right along,' he said.

'Don't have Rennit in until she arrives,' said Paul, and with a shrug of his shoulders Benson gave the necessary order.

They had to wait nearly three-quarters of an hour before Mary Henley arrived. She still looked pale, but much better for her rest. Paul apologised for having disturbed her.

'I expect you've heard of the tragedy in your house,' he ended.

'Yes, I was terribly surprised — though Irene has been peculiar lately,' she answered.

'You were friends, weren't you?' asked Rivington.

'Yes, very good friends,' replied Mary. 'We used to share meals together and buy each other's clothes, and you know the sort of thing.'

'I know,' said Paul, and his eyes gleamed.

He made a sign to Benson, and the captain pressed a bell. The next moment Dick Rennit entered in charge of two guards. He gave an exclamation as he caught sight of the girl, and his haggard face went grey.

'What's she doing here?' he muttered.

'Sit down, Rennit,' said Paul. 'We've brought you here to tell you that you're free. We've got the person who killed Lamont — she's confessed.'

Rennit gave a great cry, and his eyes flew to Mary Henley.

'She's lying!' he shouted wildly. 'She's lying. I've told you I killed Lamont. She had nothing to do with it.'

'Who do you think I mean?' said Paul in pretended surprise. 'I'm not referring to Miss Henley, if that's what you think. I'm talking about Irene Claremont.'

'Irene Claremont?' muttered Dick in a dazed way. 'Irene Claremont? What's she got to do with it?'

'She killed Lamont,' said Paul, and picked up the letter which the woman had written before taking her life. 'Apparently he'd grown tired of her, and on that night when she went to see him at the studios — they always used to use that as a meeting place — he told her so, and in a fit of jealous rage she killed him, afterwards leaving by the way she had come, down the fire escape.'

'But — but — I don't understand.' Rennit passed his tongue over his dry lips. 'I saw Mary come out of the studios. I know it was Mary, because she was wearing her red costume — '

'I sold that two days before the murder,' broke in Mary Henley, 'to Irene.'

'You made a mistake, Mr. Rennit,' said Paul gently. 'It was Irene Claremont whom you saw,'

'A mistake?' Dick Rennit looked about him dazedly. 'A mistake — '

He swayed in his chair as his overstrained nerves gave way, and Paul sprang forward just in time to prevent him slipping to the floor in a faint.

So the million-dollar film mystery came to an end, and the final threads were knotted when a search of Irene Claremont's apartment brought to light a diary which the dead girl had apparently kept partially up to date. Some of the entries were set forth at great length; others were mere scraps of almost incoherent words and phrases. But from it Paul Rivington and Captain Benson were able to piece together the whole rather sordid story. She had been very friendly with Lamont, and had at one time been under the impression that this friendship would lead to marriage. Her thoughts, set down in the little book, showed how gradually the film-editor had tired. One passage, dated four days before the murder, spoke eloquently of her state of mind:

'I went to see Perry by the usual way last night, but he wouldn't let me stay longer than two minutes. I could see that he was anxious to get rid of me, and although he pleaded pressure of work on the film, I don't believe this was the real reason. I'm sure that he was expecting someone else. I accused him of this, but he denied it. If this should be true, and there is somebody else, I swear I will do something desperate. If he's going to throw me over after all this time he shall be made to suffer for it . . . '

*　*　*

Another passage dated two days before the murder ran:

'Last night I got the truth out of him — they say that drunken men speak the truth, and Perry had been drinking. He told me to my face that he was sick of the sight of me. If I had had a weapon with me I would have killed him then. Mary has completely turned his head; it's not her fault, and, of course, it won't last. And my day is finished. I was a fool ever to think otherwise. Why do I care so much . . . '

*　*　*

And then the last entry:

'I'm going to do it tonight; I've been thinking about it all day. I shall go to the studios and make my way up to Perry's room by the fire escape as usual, and I shall take with me the pistol. He's not going to treat me as he treated all the others; I've too much respect for myself. Nobody will suspect me, and he isn't fit to live. How surprised he'll be. When I told him the other night what I'd do he only laughed at me. He won't laugh tonight . . .'

'Undoubtedly, brooding over her troubles had unbalanced the woman's mind,' said Paul, 'but there's no doubt at all now what happened. She went to the studios and killed Lamont on the night that Guinan and his partner planned the film robbery. According to Guinan they found the body when they broke in, and got the shock of their lives. But it didn't keep them from stealing the negative, which, by the irony of fate, was stolen from them by Tommy Spearman, who must have overheard the plot.'

'Well, the whole thing's over,' said Elmer Myers with a sigh of relief, 'and I guess I'm darned grateful to you, Rivington, for what you've done. If it hadn't been for you there would be no Mammoth Pictures Inc. at this moment.'

'Very nice of you to say so, Myers,' answered the detective, 'but I did very little.'

'By the way, Elmer,' said Frank Leyland, 'I'm arranging for that girl, Henley, to have a film test as you asked me.'

'Fine!' said Mr. Myers. 'If it comes out OK we might give her the second part in that new picture. By the time she's finished her honeymoon we could be ready to shoot.'

'When are they getting married?' asked Paul Rivington.

'The day after tomorrow,' answered Myers. 'They've invited me to go along. And they asked me if you and your brother would come too.'

'We'll be delighted,' said Paul. 'Then I'm afraid we shall have to say farewell to Hollywood and get back to England.'

'Say, you must stay for the premiere,' said Elmer Myers, 'You've just got to do that. I'm telling you, this is just the greatest picture that has even been shot. It'll make all the other reels of celluloid look like chunk stuff. Yes, sir, we've got the goods; we're going to make the whole world blink.'

Paul smiled.

'You beat your own advertising man at the game, Myers,' he said. 'It's very nice of you to ask us to stay, and I must say that I would like to see the picture, because, after all that has happened, I feel a personal interest in it.'

'That's swell,' said Elmer Myers. 'We're showing the picture next week at the Rialto, and in the meanwhile we'll try and give you and Bob a dandy time.'

Mr. Myers kept his word. He gave them a dandy time. He took them to Agua Caliente, over the Mexican border, to see the racing at one of the most beautiful race-courses in the world. He took them here, there and everywhere, and time seemed to fly on oiled wheels.

Then came the great night of the premiere presentation of Mammoth Pictures' super-film. Paul Rivington and Bob had visited many first nights in London and New York, but never in their lives had they seen anything to equal this one. The theatre was ablaze from foundation to roof with myriads of electric light globes and neon signs. Outside, the streets were crowded and about two hundred police-men were on duty patrolling the traffic and the people, who were lined six deep on the sidewalk for over a quarter of a mile to see the elite of the film world pass.

Those that were celebrities paused before entering the theatre and made a little speech into the microphone which was broadcast through loudspeakers to the waiting crowd. And as each world-famous star was recog-nised there went up from the massed crowd a roar of applause. Inside the theatre every seat was occupied, and Paul and Bob gazed with interest down on the sea of faces, recognising in nearly everyone features that the illustrated press of the world had made famous. Never before under one roof had they seen such a gathering of celebrities.

The entertainment was due to begin at half-past eight, and actually began at a quarter-past nine. There was a sort of preliminary to the big event of the evening — the screening of the million-dollar film. At half-past eleven there was an interval, and at a quarter to twelve the lights went down. The curtains covering the silver sheet parted slowly and the music rose to a crescendo of sound, and —

**MAMMOTH PTICTIRES
INC. PRESENTS**

appeared on the screen. This was followed by:

**THE MAN-GOD [DIRECTED BY
FRANK LEYLAND]**

After this came a whole list of names: the stars, the cameramen, the scenario writers, the scene designer, and a dozen others, and then the picture began. Paul Rivington and his brother watched it with interest, and before it was halfway through the detective had come to the conclusion that none of Mr. Elmer Myers's superlatives was an exaggeration. It was a symphony of sight and sound, conceived and executed by sheer genius. The huge audience sat tense and silent until the final fade-out. And then it rose *en masse* and cheered.

'Hear 'em,' said the delighted Mr. Myers, his face beaming. 'And they're hard-boiled. What'll it be like when it's shown to an unsophisticated audience?'

He turned away to receive the congratulations which were being showered on him, and by the time he had left the theatre and made his way to his waiting car his arm and hand were almost numb from handshakes.

'Gee, but that's one of the swellest premieres I've ever seen,' he confided to Paul Rivington; and the other agreed.

The reception that followed was a brilliant affair. Many of the celebrities had been present in the theatre who had been invited. The big ballroom at the Palace Hotel, which Mr. Myers had rented for the occasion, presented a scene of gaiety and happiness. Many were the speeches made and many the toasts drunk, and at last, in reply to cries of 'Speech,' Mr. Myers got heavily to his feet.

'This,' he began, 'is an occasion of great happiness for me. Although tonight everything has gone so smoothly and so well, few of you here realise the difficulties with which we have had to contend to make tonight possible. I do not propose to discuss these difficulties in detail; it will be sufficient if I say that at one time Mammoth Pictures Inc. was faced with complete obliteration. It is, I think, an open secret that for a long time we had fought against adverse circumstances which were brought about by a person who would have reaped considerable benefit from our downfall. But all this is a thing of the past. The fact remains that we have succeeded and the production of this film will see Mammoth Pictures supreme in the film history. We have had our financial difficulties and we have weathered them. Many toasts have been drunk this evening. I should like to propose another one. To my English friend, who made tonight possible.'

When the cheers had died away Paul Rivington rose to his feet and thanked his host.

'And there is one other toast I should like to propose,' he said gravely, 'and only a few of you who are present will fully appreciate it.' He raised his glass. 'To a very gallant gentleman,' he said.

Those who knew to whom he referred drank the toast standing.

THE END

THE FACELESS ONES
GRIM DEATH
MURDER IN MANUSCRIPT
THE GLASS ARROW
THE THIRD KEY
THE ROYAL FLUSH MURDERS
THE SQUEALER
MR. WHIPPLE EXPLAINS
THE SEVEN CLUES
THE CHAINED MAN
THE HOUSE OF THE GOAT
THE FOOTBALL POOL MURDERS
THE HAND OF FEAR
SORCERER'S HOUSE
THE HANGMAN

We do hope that you have enjoyed reading this large print book.

Did you know that all of our titles are available for purchase?

We publish a wide range of high quality large print books including:

Romances, Mysteries, Classics
General Fiction
Non Fiction and Westerns

Special interest titles available in large print are:

The Little Oxford Dictionary
Music Book, Song Book
Hymn Book, Service Book

Also available from us courtesy of Oxford University Press:

Young Readers' Dictionary
(large print edition)
Young Readers' Thesaurus
(large print edition)

For further information or a free brochure, please contact us at:

Ulverscroft Large Print Books Ltd.,
The Green, Bradgate Road, Anstey,
Leicester, LE7 7FU, England.
Tel: (00 44) **0116 236 4325**
Fax: (00 44) **0116 234 0205**

STORM EVIL

John Robb

A terrible storm sweeps across a vast desert of North Africa. Five legionnaires and a captain on a training course are caught in it and take refuge in a ruined temple. Into the temple, too, come four Arabs laden with hate for the Legion captain. Then a beautiful aviator arrives — the estranged wife of the officer. When darkness falls, and the storm rages outside, the Arabs take a slow and terrible vengeance against the captain. Death strikes suddenly, often, and in a grotesque form . . .